2 Novella-Length

VISIT
FROM
BEYOND!

2 Novella-Length

VISIT FROM BEYOND!

From The Editors
Of *True Story* And
True Confessions

Published by True Renditions, LLC

True Renditions, LLC
105 E. 34th Street, Suite 141
New York, NY 10016

ISBN: 978-1-938877-69-8

Visit us on the web at www.truerenditionsllc.com.

Contents

Book-Length Visit From Beyond!

DON JUAN'S TENDER TURNAROUND

He had to almost die to learn how to live

"I think the doctor removed your funny bone when you were in the hospital," Lauren said. She chewed her lip and met my gaze. "Seriously, Joe—you haven't been the same since the accident."

This wasn't the first time I heard that remark from my girlfriend or other friends. They were right; I wasn't the same after I almost died in that car accident. Gone was the fun-loving guy who lived in my skin for twenty-five years and in his place was a confused young man who questioned everything in his life.

Lauren plopped down next to me on the sofa, letting a small sigh escape from her lips. "It's all because of that dream," she said in an accusing tone. "It's still bugging you, isn't it?"

I wanted to tell her that she was wrong, but I couldn't lie. "It was so real," I said as my mind instantly began replaying my dream.

"It was just a dream, Joe—probably brought on by the pain medication," she said, not even trying to conceal her exasperation. "You just need to forget about it."

As though I haven't tried, I thought in frustration. No matter what I did I couldn't erase the image of my grandfather from my mind. Even then, as I talked with Lauren, I could see the dream in my mind's eye; Granddad was standing in a white light so bright that it was almost blinding, dressed for work in his favorite, navy-blue suit, crisp, white shirt, and striped tie. His hair was dark brown and thick and he stood tall and strong like he was before he got cancer and died. "Joe," he asked in his deep, sonorous voice, "what are you doing with your life?" Then the dream ended with me, dry-mouthed, trying to form an answer to his question.

I know some people put a lot of meaning into dreams, believing they foretell the future or are messages from the beyond. Not me. Until this point. Since the dream I kept having the uneasy feeling that Granddad was looking down at me from heaven. And that he was disappointed.

"Right now we need to watch our movie." Lauren turned on the DVD player where she'd loaded The Empire Strikes Back, picked out just for me. "Maybe spending more time with your friends will perk you up," she suggested. "Remember how much fun we had at your birthday party?"

1

I nodded. Looking back, my party seemed decades ago instead of only a few weeks before my accident. As for perking me up—I didn't know what I needed to give me mental peace or to turn me back into the carefree guy I used to be, but I doubted an evening with my friends spent downing brews and dancing all night was the ticket.

I gazed at Lauren's serious, brown eyes as she hit the PLAY button on the remote. She and I were only dating for four months when a semi slid on a patch of ice and slammed into my Camero, totaling it and sending me to the hospital for three weeks. Lauren's typical of the girls I like to date—sexy and always looking for a good time. She has long, curly, black hair and curvy hips and full breasts that even her conservative supermarket uniform can't conceal. Best of all, she has a thirst for fun without any commitment. She spent her teenage years raising her two sisters and a brother, so she has no interest in marriage or children for years to come. She just wants to enjoy her freedom and catch up on the fun she missed.

Although our relationship was never serious, she'd come to the hospital every day, always bringing me magazines, snacks, and other gifts to cheer me up. As much as I looked forward to seeing her cute smile and mischievous, brown eyes, it was Sabrina Mayhew I wanted to see most every day. Sabrina was one of the nurses who took care of me.

Sabrina and I actually went to high school together, but I never paid much attention to her for a couple of reasons. In the first place, we hung out with different crowds. Although I was always a good student I liked fast cars, wild parties, and cute girls out for a good time. Sabrina never went to parties and she spent most of her time preoccupied with honor society activities or in the library with her nose in a book. Secondly, Sabrina was never much to look at; she wore heavy, brown-framed glasses, matronly clothes, and her blond hair was always stringy and dull. Behind her back my buddy, Josh, called her Owl Eyes—very appropriate.

One of the first lessons I learned in the hospital is that time can change people. When I woke up in my hospital bed I didn't recognize the nurse with the sparkling eyes and shining hair piled on top of her head. But she recognized me right away.

"It's about time you woke up; you've been sleeping for two days." Her voice was soft and gently teasing as she looked across the bed at the other nurse who was pumping up the blood pressure cuff on my arm. "Joe and I went to Hamilton High together," she explained.

My mind was fuzzy but I was able to make out the name on her identification tag: Sabrina Mayhew. The nurse was Sabrina, all grown up.

Over the next three weeks I found out that there is a whole lot more to Sabrina than her new looks. She has a sense of humor that makes her patients smile even through their pain, she never complains about so much as a patient's smallest request, and she has the kindest heart I've ever known.

At the time, she also had a boyfriend—some guy named Matthew who I figured was probably a George Clooney look-alike. Sabrina's a nurse, after all, so it only made sense to me that she'd be dating a doctor—someone like Clooney with bedroom eyes, thick, black hair, and broad shoulders bursting out of his white lab coat. As it was, the nurses were always asking her about him and it seemed to me like they went everywhere together—movies, dinners, and the park. And probably to bed, although of course she didn't talk about that.

"Do you want some more popcorn?" Lauren asked as she held out the empty bowl. I jerked my thoughts back to Lauren, where they belonged, and agreed that more popcorn was a good idea.

Once the movie ended, I pushed myself up from the sofa. "I think I'll make it an early night," I said. "Tomorrow's a work day." I'd returned to work the week before, but was still only working half-days.

"Is your leg bothering you?" Lauren asked as she stood up beside me.

"Some," I said, although my leg actually felt pretty good that day and I wasn't even using the crutches anymore. The truth is, I was just ready to leave, I guess. The earlier talk about my dream had made it hard for me to concentrate on the movie and my mind was still churning over Granddad, Sabrina, and my hospital experiences.

Lauren gave me an understanding smile and wrapped her arms around my neck. "You went through a lot with the accident," she said. "Pretty soon, though, you'll be your old self and we can have fun again." She rubbed her breasts against my chest and giggled; Lauren especially loved turning up the heat in the bedroom, something we hadn't done since my accident. A broken leg and the incision running down my abdomen had slowed down my zest for making love, even to a firecracker like Lauren.

Funny thing, actually: I didn't miss our hot-and-sweaty lovemaking sessions, but I knew that she did. So I enveloped her in my arms and met her lips with mine. They were soft and warm and her tongue gently teased mine as she held me tighter. It was a kiss filled with an open invitation for a whole lot more, but like everything else in my life at that point, the kiss just didn't feel "right" to me.

When I got home I popped open a beer and sank into the recliner in front of the TV. Thanks to Lauren my apartment sparkled from top to bottom; over the weekend she'd vacuumed, mopped the kitchen floor, and changed my bed linens—all tasks that were still hard for me to do because of my leg. I picked up the John Grisham novel I'd started to read the night before and flipped it open to the bookmarked page. I was never much of a reader until Harry Nelson became my hospital roommate; Harry changed my attitude about a lot of things.

When the stretcher carrying that silver-haired gentleman was wheeled into my hospital room, I immediately thought he'd be a boring roommate because of the difference in our ages. The nurses had barely settled Harry into his bed when his family began to arrive; there was his wife, Ann, plus two sons in there thirties and their wives. In our small room it was impossible not to observe them and overhear their conversations. Whenever Harry was with them his whole face literally glowed with happiness even though I knew he was in pain from his cancer surgery. The family's love for one another was as powerful as the sun and filled the room with warmth I'd never experienced before. They even pulled me into their circle by including me in their conversations, watching TV shows together, and lending me books to read, like the Grisham novel I was reading. Of course, everything I observed or heard wasn't all smiles and laughter. There were hushed moments when Harry and Ann whispered about his cancer and the biopsy reports. But to me, those discussions were even more powerful and poignant than the happy moments.

My relationship with my parents wasn't at all like what Harry and his family had. My dad married my mom because she got pregnant with me—a fact my dad constantly brought up, even in my presence. My parents didn't talk to each other—they argued with angry voices. When I was ten, Dad finally moved out, announcing that he was marrying someone he'd met at work—a woman who wasn't forcing him to the altar. He remarried and moved several states away, never to be heard from again.

After Dad left, Mom went through a string of lousy relationships until she married Roger, the man of her dreams. While Roger was crazy about Mom, those feelings didn't carry over toward me; Roger didn't like kids and having me around put a real strain on their relationship. One day I was talking to Granddad about Mom's marriage to Roger and I let it slip that it was stressful for them when I was around. The next thing I knew I was moving into Granddad's house with Mom's blessing and Roger's silent sigh of relief. Granddad and I always got along and since his divorce he lived alone, so even when Mom and Roger got divorced a couple of years later I didn't move back home. I'd settled in with Granddad and he said I could stay.

Don't get me wrong—life with Granddad wasn't total bliss; he was a serious man with strict morals and a strong sense of purpose. He was the principal of my high school and his job was very demanding. He worked every day and at all hours, and at night and on the weekends he attended long meetings, worked on the skimpy school budget, and fretted about students who were in trouble. His blood pressure ran sky high, he was overweight, and his face was lined with tension and worry for as long as I can remember.

Around about my junior year I guess I decided that I didn't want a life like his, so I focused my attention in school on having a good time. He used to preach to me about the importance of good grades, getting into a good college, and having a notable career—all stuff that led to a heavy life like his, as far as I could see. Still, by the time I graduated I'd decided that I'd at least go to a junior college to make Granddad happy and to get a job that would pay my bills and put beer in the fridge. I wasn't ever going to get married, though. As it was, as I celebrated my graduation and newfound freedom, Mom was on her fourth marriage and it was floundering. Everywhere I looked, people were either unhappy in their marriages or getting divorced, so I couldn't see that marriage offered anyone that much, anyway. And I already knew that you don't have to be married to have sex, so what more was there? For five years I'd been happy sitting next to Josh, writing web pages for the county health department and having two or three new girlfriends a year. I didn't keep girlfriends long because they always broke up with me since I wasn't the marrying kind.

But since that dream I wondered about my life. What do I have? I'd ask myself. Oh, I definitely had friends—friends to have fun with. Every day I was in the hospital some of them would come to visit and gather around my bed telling jokes and stories, but when they were there I didn't feel love like I felt from Harry's side of the room. As for work, I had a job, but I didn't talk about it with enthusiasm the way Harry talked about his accounting practice. I had Lauren, but I didn't have strong feelings for her. I guess you could say that all in all, my life was kind of empty, even though it was full.

I saw Granddad in my dream—tall, strong, and dressed for a day behind the principal's desk. It was so like him to ask me what I was doing with my life; he was always asking me things like that. I know it's crazy, but I felt like he spoke to me from heaven. It's like I was given a second chance with my life since I came through the accident alive and in one piece—a chance to make the most of my life. But no one else felt the way I did. Lauren thought my dream was simply due to me being under the influence of powerful painkillers and sedatives and was no big deal. When I told Mom about it, she laughed and said, "Sounds like something your grandfather would say if he were still with us."

Josh shook his head when I told him about it. "Too bad you didn't dream about Angelina Jolie or some other hot chick."

I took a swig of my now-warm beer and gazed at the crutches

leaning against the wall near the front door. Sabrina had told me that I could return them at the hospital equipment rental office, but suddenly I realized that I wanted to see her again—when I wasn't flat on my back in a faded hospital nightgown—so I decided I'd take them to the floor where she worked. I planned to arrive at twelve-thirty, when she goes to lunch. Even though she had Matthew in her life, I still wanted to talk with her again—to see her violet eyes and warm smile and hear her infectious laugh.

"There's a web consultant position open," I told Josh the next day as I looked through the weekly posting of job openings at the health department.

He just shrugged and continued typing code into his computer for the web program he was working on.

"I might apply," I added as I studied the posting.

The sound of Josh's tapping on the keyboard stopped and the cubicle space we shared became quiet. I looked up from the posting and at Josh. He was staring at me like I'd grown another head.

"You know what those consultants do. Why would you want to do that?"

By "that," he meant meet with department managers, work with staff committees, and implement web pages on time and to the manager's satisfaction. Previously, I'd always said that a consultant's job wasn't worth the few extra bucks I'd make doing it. As it was my current job met my bill requirements, kept me stocked with beer, and didn't follow me home at night, so why ask for more headaches and more work—right? But suddenly I was thinking differently. Wondering if perhaps I should be looking for more challenging work.

"Dude, are you still taking those painkillers?" Josh asked.

I shook my head. "Nope. Why?"

He shrugged and started typing again. "Just wondered. You're not yourself anymore. The old Joe wouldn't have given that job posting a second glance." He turned his chair toward me and leaned forward. "It's not just the announcement, dude—it's everything. Like last week, you were like a silent stranger at Jeff's party. Everyone was having a good time and you were just sitting there like a quiet observer."

What he said was true. I couldn't get into the party groove that night; Lauren wasn't happy with me, either. She wanted to dance and I couldn't because of my leg; she wanted to drink and get loose and I didn't. To further complicate the evening, my thoughts kept returning to my dream and my grandfather's question. I kept toying with that question while everyone danced and Lauren downed drink after drink on top of too many.

"I've been doing a lot of thinking since the accident about what

I want out of life," I explained to Josh with a kind of embarrassed shrug.

"I thought we figured that out years ago," he said. "We both watched your grandfather and my folks work night and day and never enjoy their lives, but we've both got just exactly what we want—stable jobs and girlfriends who aren't into heavy relationships. What more do you want?"

He was right; I did have what I wanted. In fact, the thought occurred to me, I should be happy instead of confused.

"Joe! You're walking on your own!" Sabrina greeted me as she and several other nurses grouped around me. I leaned my crutches against the counter of the nurse's station and held up my arms and walked in a little circle. Everyone laughed and applauded.

A minute ago when I'd spotted Sabrina's smiling face in the nurse's station, my heart sped up and all of a sudden I felt like a hot-blooded teenager. Her turquoise scrubs were as elegant as any evening gown and she looked absolutely beautiful to me. My heart was still racing as I talked with everyone; I was so happy to see her that I had to fight the impulse to give her a hug. After several minutes of conversation, all of the nurses except Sabrina scattered off to various

"I'm glad to see you're doing so well," Sabrina said, "but you could've saved yourself a long walk by returning the crutches on the first floor."

"I wanted to see you," I told her. "I thought maybe we could grab some lunch downstairs." I would've suggested something nicer, but I knew she didn't have time to leave the hospital for lunch.

"Don't tell me you've missed the hospital food!" she teased.

Just you, I thought. I grinned. "Maybe it tastes better eaten at a table instead of in bed."

She shook her head. "Not much, but there's a deli bar in the cafeteria where we can get sandwiches."

"Sabrina, Matthew's on the phone." The receptionist held up the telephone receiver as she called to Sabrina. Her words spoiled the mood and reminded me that Sabrina had a George Clooney in her life.

"Tell him I'll call him back," Sabrina said.

As we walked to the elevator I had to bite my tongue to keep from asking her about Matthew; after all, I knew he was none of my business. Downstairs at the deli bar in the cafeteria we both ordered turkey-and-cranberry sandwiches with sides of macaroni salad and root beers and then we found a vacant table by the windows. Once seated, teenage feelings of being tongue-tied and self-conscious flooded through me as I wondered, why did I ask her to lunch? She's dating Matthew and she's definitely not the type of girl I usually date, anyway; she's way too serious about life.

"Are you working yet?" she asked me as she tucked into her macaroni salad.

"I went back last week; I'm working half-days now, but I start full time next week."

"Even half-days can be tiring. Getting around on crutches isn't easy; plus, surgery really saps your energy."

I hadn't planned to talk about my medical condition, so when she paused I quickly changed the subject. "When did you decide to go into nursing?"

"Oh, I've wanted this for as long as I can remember." She smiled and her eyes sparkled. "When I was a little girl my mom and I visited my grandmother in the nursing home every Sunday. I'd watch the nurses working and think about how wonderful it'd be to wear a cap and white uniform. Of course, that was years ago—back when nurses wore caps and uniforms starched so heavily that they crackled when they walked." She chuckled. "And then there was the money, too."

"Money?"

She nodded. "My dad died when I was little and Mom never made much money at the restaurant where she worked. I wanted a job where I could make money to buy things that weren't from Goodwill and so that I wouldn't cry over bills like my mom always did."

"How did you afford nursing school?"

"It wasn't easy. In high school I worked nights and weekends at the nursing home where my grandmother lived. I saved every penny I earned toward college and I also got a couple of small scholarships."

As she spoke I remembered her being in the honor society and always studying in the library when the rest of us were goofing off. Her life was never easy, I could tell, but her efforts had obviously paid off. I pictured the girl I knew back in high school with her heavy, framed glasses, odd clothes, and stringy hair; I began to see her in a different light and had a better understanding of what lay behind her physical appearance. Sadly, I knew my friends and I weren't very kind or understanding back in high school.

"You said you work for the county health department?" she asked as she took a sip of her root beer.

I nodded. "In the web group." I told her about my job and how I took programming classes at the junior college. Of course, I left out the part about wanting a job that paid the rent and for beer, but caused no headaches. "Actually, I'm thinking about applying for a job with broader responsibilities." I surprised myself by saying this to her because I honestly wasn't trying to impress her; it's just that she was so easy to talk with that the words came right out of me.

"What would you be doing?" There was genuine interest in her pretty eyes and voice.

I explained a bit about the job and finished with, "I'm still trying to make up my mind about applying."

She nodded sympathetically. "Changing jobs is a big decision and you've been through a lot these past few weeks."

"Yeah, but I'm feeling pretty strong now," I said, thinking she meant that I was still physically weak from my surgeries.

"Oftentimes it takes longer for the emotional wounds to heal," she said as she set down her root beer. "Being in a car accident is a very traumatic experience—at best. I had a patient tell me that when a car slammed into her convertible, she felt like her whole life passed before her eyes and she thought she knew in that instant that she was going to die. It took her months to get over that memory."

I nodded grimly. "It's a terrible feeling," I admitted. As it was, I still shuddered every time I drove by the intersection on Barker Road where the semi hit me.

"Some people have emotional issues that last for months after an accident. They can't sleep; they have trouble driving—trouble just functioning from day to day."

"I'm doing okay that way," I said. "The only thing that sticks in my mind is a dream I had about my grandfather right before I woke up."

Her eyes perked up. "Tell me about it."

I recalled everyone else's reaction to my dream and instantly regretted bringing it up. But it was too late then, so I told her about it. "Anyway," I said dismissively when I'd recounted the incident, "it was probably induced by all the pain medication I was on at the time."

She considered this. "That could be it. Or it could be something else. Some people experience what are called NDEs or Near Death Experiences when they're in accidents or come very close to dying. Sometimes people see relatives who've passed away and catch a glimpse of the afterlife. The experiences can be very life-altering." She went on to explain various explanations for these events, ranging from paranormal phenomena to chemical reactions in the brain.

I shook my head. "I've never heard of anything like that before, but I don't think that's what happened to me."

"Perhaps not, but your dream can still have an emotional impact. It was probably unsettling and could cause you to view your life differently from now on."

I didn't want to talk about myself, but suddenly I was glad that I brought up my dream. Finally, someone understood what I was feeling. I was just starting to ask her a few questions when her pager went off, bringing our conversation to an abrupt halt. She glanced down at her message screen and her eyes turned dark as she frowned.

"There's an emergency on the floor," she said as she pushed back her chair and stood. "I'm sorry, but I've got to go right away."

I didn't want her to leave; I felt like I was just getting to know her. But she started to pick up her tray.

"You go on ahead," I said. "I'll take care of that for you."

"Thanks for lunch," she called as she turned to head for the exit. I stood watching her as she raced away with her pretty hair bouncing.

"Web consultant is the next logical promotion for a web programmer," my boss, Jim Carter, said. He frowned and paused as though gathering his thoughts.

Jim had been my boss ever since I started with the county health department and I always liked his straightforward approach to things. He was old enough to be my father, but never acted fatherly; he always treated his employees like he was the coach and we were his winning team. I'd decided to tell him that I was interested in the consultant job to see if I could get his support; however, by the hesitation in his voice I had the feeling that no support would be forthcoming.

"I hear a 'but' coming," I said, trying to lighten the heavy air in the room.

Jim gave me a small smile as he rested his elbows on his desk. "First of all, I'm glad to see that you're interested in doing more than writing programs. You're a smart guy and I think you've been sitting on your potential. On the other hand, you haven't taken any classes or volunteered for any projects to give you the skills that you need for a consulting job. I've got five other employees who're eager to become consultants and they've all taken classes to help them get there."

The more he talked, the more I knew he was right; I never took any classes unless the department required it, and as for volunteering for special projects—I never gave the notion a second thought because I always figured it'd cut into my free time.

"I guess I need to start taking some classes, then." My words sounded lame, but at least they made sense.

Jim nodded. "That's a good start. Bear in mind, though, that with the budget cuts, I can only send a few people to classes. I have to give priority to employees who are in special projects or who've already got classes under their belts."

Another blow, which shouldn't have surprised me. Somehow, it seemed only fitting that when I finally decided to take a leap forward, all the doors were closed and locked to me, or at least hard to open.

When I got back to my desk I told Josh about my conversation with Jim. "I don't think you'd like that work, anyway," he rationalized.

He talked for a few minutes about how consulting jobs are lots of work and headaches and while I agreed with everything he said, I still felt like I'd like to give it a try. I was still mulling over the consultant job when he switched topics.

"You and Lauren are coming tonight, aren't you?" It was Friday night and we always met at the Starlight Tavern to shoot pool, dance, eat wings, and down several pitchers.

"Yeah, we'll be there. Lauren's not working tonight."

I wished she was working so that I could stay home, but I knew she'd switched shifts with another clerk at the Thriftway so she could get off. I'd been questioning my feelings for Lauren ever since the accident, but my concerns ran even deeper after having lunch with Sabrina. Still, I figured I had about as much chance of getting a date with Sabrina as I did of getting a consulting job; after all, she had Matthew in her life.

I flipped off my computer and stood up. It was my last half-day before I returned to working full time and I intended to use my afternoon to return Harry's books to him. His wife had been so nice to bring me stacks of novels to read while I recuperated that I wanted to show my appreciation by returning them promptly. As it was, when Ann gave me the books I thought I'd have enough to read for years, but I surprised myself and plowed through them in record time. Of course, I was spending more evenings at home and not out at the bars with Lauren or Josh like I used to. Anyway, it would be nice to see Harry again; I'd enjoyed his company in the hospital and missed his lively comments during the news and Law & Order reruns.

Harry welcomed me with a hearty handshake and showed me into his private office. On his desk were several framed pictures of Ann and his two boys—at the beach, gathered around a campfire in lawn chairs, and in front of a Christmas tree. Harry immediately plunged into telling me his good news.

"No chemo and no radiation." His face was all smiles and the sparkle in his gray eyes made him look younger than his years. "The doctor believes the surgery got all of the cancer."

"That's great news, Harry." I knew he'd been worried about the biopsy report; in fact, I'd been concerned about it, too. I didn't want him to go through the trials of cancer treatment like Granddad did.

"How are you doing?" he asked. "Walking without crutches, I see."

I nodded and grinned. "I returned them to the hospital yesterday."

"So your body's healing well, then. And how about the mind? A car accident isn't something a person forgets right away."

"That's definitely true; I'll never feel the same way about Barker Road again." I laughed, trying not to make too big a deal out of it.

"Seriously, Joe—an accident like yours can mess with a person's head. I saw it in Vietnam with guys who got shot." He paused and toyed with a small notepad on his desk. "It happened to me when I was over there."

"Really?" I couldn't imagine him being anything but all together.

He shrugged. "I don't talk about it much." His gray eyes darkened for a moment and then he continued, "My best buddy and I were in combat over there and we both got shot. I made it; he didn't."

The subject was so serious that I didn't know what to say, so I simply nodded and listened as he talked about waking up in a field hospital in horrible pain and asking about his friend, only to learn that he'd died before they got him into the chopper.

"Afterward, I started questioning a lot of things in my life. At the time, my life wasn't really headed anywhere; I got drafted right out of high school and I didn't have a clue about what I was going to do when I got home. But after Mike died, I got to thinking about how life can be so short and wondering if I was making the most of it. It took me a while to figure out what I wanted to do, but when I left Nam I had plans for the next phase of my life."

"I've had some similar thoughts," I admitted, blushing a little, though I honestly don't know why.

"Watching a semi head straight for you can do that, kiddo."

I nodded. "I still think about the accident a lot, but what I can't forget is a dream I had about my grandfather." I quickly added that I didn't believe in dreams foretelling the future and stuff like that.

"Even so," he said, "the dream must've been very impressive to stick in your mind like it has. Tell me about it."

Harry's eyes were rapt with attention as he asked me question after question and I gradually told him about the dream and my life with Granddad. Unlike my conversation with Sabrina, I told him about how I'd tailored my life in a direction far different from my grandfather's way of living.

"Sounds like you had a wakeup call and need to look at your life," Harry surmised. He shrugged. "Perhaps some changes are in order."

I gave a bitter laugh. "Everything I'm thinking of changing is impossible." I told him about my conversation with Jim.

"Are you serious about this new job?"

I nodded, raking a hand through my hair. "I think so, but there's no way I'll get any training because of the budget cutbacks."

"Can you get the training on your own? Like at the junior college?"

"Well . . . yeah." I blushed a little. "I hadn't thought of that."

He nodded. "It'll cost you some money and cut into your free time, but it would really show your boss just how interested and committed you are. Maybe if you take a couple of classes on your own, your boss will investigate and somehow 'find' money for you to take other classes."

I had to admit that his idea had real merit. As it was, I'd saved some money that I knew I could use for the tuition. By taking a couple of classes I'd also have a better idea about whether or not consulting was really the type of work I wanted to do. The more I thought about it, the more I liked the idea.

"So? What else is impossible?" Harry asked, cutting into my thoughts.

I shrugged and managed a rueful grin. "That's about it," I said, not wanting to sing the blues about Sabrina and Matthew. But as usual, Harry was one step ahead of me.

"Did you ever ask out that cute little nurse? The one you went to high school with?"

I felt myself blushing as I grinned.

Harry smiled and chuckled. "I could tell she had your eye."

"She is cute. In fact . . . I took her to lunch when I brought back my crutches."

"And?"

"And she's got a boyfriend." I shrugged. "She's never talked about him, but I know she got a call from him while I was there." I pictured her again with a George Clooney-style doctor—tall and dark-haired with a sexy, knees-weakening smile.

"You might still want to ask her out, kiddo; it certainly can't hurt to ask." He grinned. "She might even say yes, Joe."

Before I left Harry offered to help me with my income taxes for free and told me he'd call when he had more books to loan me. By then it was early afternoon and I started to head home. When I saw the sign for the junior college, I changed my mind and drove onto the campus. The spring quarter was starting soon and I figured I might be able to get into a night class.

"You're going to night school?"

Josh's eyes looked like they were going to pop right out of his head. He grimaced, lifted his pint glass of Bud, and took a swig. Lauren sat next to me with a puzzled look on her face; we were at the Starlight with Josh and his girlfriend, Mindy. We were all talking while the house band took a break.

"What class are you taking?" Lauren asked.

"Actually, I'm taking two—"

"Two?" Josh interrupted.

I nodded. "Fundamentals of Consulting Part One and Planning Functional Websites." I'd only planned to take one class, but when I looked at the course descriptions I decided to go for both. That way, I figured I'd quickly find out if a consulting job was something I really was interested in or just a wild idea.

"I think that accident gave you a personality change," Josh said as he refilled his glass and motioned for the waitress to bring us another pitcher of beer.

"You haven't been the same," Lauren quickly agreed, nodding a little too emphatically for my pleasure. Her brown eyes were serious and there was an air of sadness in them like she was losing her best . . . something.

I realized at once that she and Josh really didn't understand where I was coming from. They'd only seen my broken bones and torn-up abdomen; they didn't know what it's like to watch a semi swerve, twist, and slam broadside into you, and then have a dream with your grandfather in the starring role. The way I looked at it, though, it was no wonder that I was thinking about what I'd accomplished in my life and where I was going with the rest of it.

"I was talking with Harry Nelson and he said that an accident like mine can make a person really look at his life," I said, thinking some insight from a guy like Harry might help them understand what was happening to me. "Harry went through something like it back in Nam." I shrugged and tried to seem casual and cool, even though what I was talking about was suddenly incredibly important to me. "It's like a wakeup call."

"Whoa. All of this stuff is waaay too deep for me," Josh announced with an exaggerated sigh. "Anyway, right now I hear a dance call." His lips curled into a mischievous grin as he grabbed Mindy's hand and led her out onto the dance floor where the band was starting up again.

"You really have changed," Lauren said when we were alone at our table. "The old Joe would never spend his free time in a stuffy classroom or hang out with an accountant old enough to be his father." She bit her lip and met my gaze, studying me for my response.

I shrugged and moved my half-empty glass on the sticky table. "I guess I'm just trying to find out who I really am—who I am now, at least, post-accident."

She sat back in her chair, still studying my face intently, gauging me. "All I know is that I liked you just the way you were before the accident." She gave me a little smile and stood up. "Let's dance."

Her tight, black slacks hugged her butt as she led the way out onto the dance floor in her stiletto-heeled sandals. That night her black hair hung loose with the curls brushing the tops of her breasts. We joined the crowd on the dance floor and she wrapped her arms around my neck, settling her face close to mine.

We'd been dancing for a few minutes when she cuddled closer, lifting her lips to my ear. "How's your incision?"

I knew her question was an invitation to her bed. An invitation any man in his right mind would take. But right then I was unsure about my feelings for her and somehow it just didn't feel honorable to share her bed—not when I was thinking of Sabrina. So I lied.

"The muscles are still tender, actually."

"Maybe you'll feel better next week," she whispered, and kissed the corner of my jaw.

I hope my mind feels better next week, I thought. Right then I felt like I was in Limboland. Even hanging with my friends and my girl wasn't enjoyable like it used to be. I couldn't get Sabrina out of my mind. Going to night school was all-new territory for me. And my bachelor life, so free of commitments and strings, suddenly looked empty and lonely in the years ahead.

"This is wonderful tiramisu." Sabrina slipped her fork through the chocolaty dessert, cutting off a bite-sized piece. Like most guys I'm not too keen on gooey desserts, so I was having something simple—apple pie à la mode.

As we enjoyed our desserts I found myself feeling really glad that I'd asked Sabrina to dinner. For two weeks I'd debated with myself about asking her, plagued by fears of rejection not unlike those a teenage guy has when he asks someone out for the first time. But Harry's encouragement kept playing in my mind until I finally reached for the phone and punched in the number for the surgical wing. Once the invitation for dinner was out of my mouth, I'd gritted my teeth and told myself that if I could handle being hit by a semi I could handle a refusal, especially from someone who had a guy in her life. But Sabrina didn't refuse; she accepted. Immediately. With warmth in her voice that made me feel good all over.

I took her to The Italian Villa, an upscale restaurant that specializes in homemade pastas and fancy, decadent desserts. It's romantic, too; murals of Italy decorate the walls, soft candlelight glows on each table, and forest-green tablecloths and napkins dress each table. Sabrina fit right into her surroundings; she wore her hair down that night, letting the waves fall gently around her shoulders. Her black dress was short and it really showed off her long legs and slender waist and the neckline dipped just enough for me to catch glimpses of the tops of her breasts when she moved a certain way.

As we ate we talked about everything from The Da Vinci Code to the runaway bride. I liked talking with her; she's smart, well read, and interested in all kinds of things. Right then, I was telling her about my visit with Harry. "He's quite a guy," I told her. "Harry has a really nice family; I hope when I have kids that they grow up to be as good to me as Harry's sons are to him." I pictured Sabrina with a couple of small children at her side and all of a sudden I got a funny feeling in my gut—like she'd be a good mother and having kids with someone like her would really be something I'd like to do. I swallowed and said, "I was never around a family like his until I was in the hospital." She gave me a quizzical look, so I explained about how I'd lived with Granddad and wasn't close to my mother.

"I know it was hard for my mom when my dad died," she said, nodding in sympathy, "but there was always a lot of love between Mom and me and I was close to my grandma and my aunt and uncle." Her eyes clouded for a moment and her gaze drifted to her wineglass before she met my eyes again. "My aunt died about six months ago and my uncle's taken her death really hard. I've been spending as much time as I can with Uncle Matthew, trying to help him rebuild his life."

I barely heard her as she talked about the dinners she cooked, the movies they watched on cable, and all of the other things she did for and with Uncle Matthew. Suddenly, all I could think about was that maybe she didn't have a George Clooney in her life, after all.

"This is where your accident happened, isn't it?" Sabrina asked a while later as we drove along Barker Road to her apartment.

"The semi hit me right about here," I said, nodding. Through the light from the headlights the approaching corner looked quiet and serene, but I could still see the blinding lights of that truck cab as it turned at me and then the silver side of the truck sliding toward me.

"That had to be terrifying," she said.

I nodded. "The side of a semi never looked so big," I said, trying to keep my tone light.

"Are you still bothered by the dream you had? The one about your grandfather?"

"Some," I admitted. I was surprised that she brought up the dream; Lauren and Josh didn't like hearing about it.

"It's kind of like you got a second chance at life," she said. In the darkness of the car I couldn't see her face but I could feel the smile in her voice.

"I think I was existing before, but not really living," I admitted. "I skated along day by day, but I never really had a plan."

She turned to look at me in the darkness. "Do you have a plan now?"

I wasn't sure about how to answer that. My head was filled with thoughts of getting a better job and having a family like Harry's, but my feet were still in wet cement and I was unsteady and unsure about the changes I was making. Right then, I didn't feel comfortable in my old world or the new world I was exploring. "I guess I'm trying to figure that out," I finally said honestly.

"I was surprised that you asked me to dinner." She paused and then rushed on, "I thought that dark-haired girl who visited you in the hospital was your girlfriend."

Another tough topic. But I respected her for having the courage to bring it up. "She and I were going out before the accident. Since the accident, though, I think we're moving in different directions."

We rode quietly in the car the rest of the way to her apartment. "Do you like lasagna?" she asked when we were there and I parked and walked her to her front door.

"Uh-huh."

Her gaze met mine as we stood at her door with the bright, overhead light illuminating our faces. "Would you like to come for dinner this weekend? I make pretty good lasagna."

"I'd like that a lot," I said softly.

She smiled. "Friday, then? Saturday? Sunday? What day works best for you?"

"Sunday sounds good," I said, thinking I could do homework on Saturday. I reached down and took her hand in mine; it was warm and smooth and soft as satin and it was the first time I touched her. Not that I hadn't wanted to all that night; in the candlelight of the restaurant I couldn't keep my eyes off of her, especially her infinitely kissable mouth.

She took a small step forward, closer to me. I reached my hand behind her shoulders, pulled her closer, and leaned my head toward hers. She lifted her face to me, her lips full and soft, and I brushed my lips against hers as her silky curls fell around my fingertips. The kiss may have been light, but its impact was like a jolt from the heavens. My heart raced and thudded against my chest and the hormones that had been dormant since the accident came instantly alive and pulsed through my whole body as I kissed her again, more deeply, that time letting my tongue dip into her soft, wet mouth. After just two kisses I was ready to kiss every inch of her, but I knew it was too soon. The old me would've had her coat unbuttoned by then with my hands exploring and enjoying, but the new me reluctantly finished the kiss and then slowly drew back, folding her in my arms for a tender hug.

"I'll see you Sunday," I whispered.

As I drove home my whole body ached to finish the lovemaking we'd started. At the same time, the idea of actually having a relationship with Sabrina scared me to death. And then there was Lauren to think of; after all, she'd stood by me for weeks while I was in the hospital and had been more than patient about my slow recovery and ramblings about my dream.

The next morning I tried to fend off Josh's prodding about my date with Sabrina. I didn't plan to tell him about it, but he didn't give me much choice.

"I called you last night to see if you wanted to shoot some pool, but I guess you must've been at one of your classes," he said right away when I sat down at my desk.

17

Moments later: "You went out with Owl Eyes?" Josh's hands were suspended over his keyboard and his mouth hung open when I told him I'd taken Sabrina to The Italian Villa.

From there the conversation went downhill fast. We got into it when I told him not to call Sabrina names like "Owl Eyes" anymore; the name was hurtful and made me feel guilty for my immature thoughts years ago.

"What about Lauren?" he asked after we'd argued over the hurtful nickname.

I blushed a little and looked sheepish, instantly feeling horribly guilty. "I've got to talk to her." I raked my hands through my hair; all night I'd tossed and turned while thoughts of Lauren, Sabrina, my classes, and work churned around in my tired mind. "I thought Lauren was the kind of girl I wanted to date, but now I'm not so sure." I rattled on about how Lauren didn't want kids and how I was beginning to think I wanted more out of life than relationships with no outcome other than a good time.

Josh considered this and me, his face filling with a seriousness that I'd only seen in him a few times in my life. "You're really confused, buddy, aren't you?" His words were direct, but there was kindness in his tone.

I nodded and met his gaze, not saying anything.

He shrugged. "I'd like to help you, but I'm not sure about how to do that. One minute you're the Joe I've known for years and the next minute you're a guy I don't even recognize." He held out his hands helplessly.

"I'm sure I'll work things out on my own," I said, even though I wasn't at all sure.

I glanced at the thick, black project folder on my desk—a reminder of yet another change in my life. When I'd told Jim about taking classes on my own money, he offered me an opportunity to work on a web design project with an experienced team. I couldn't refuse, plus it was a good chance to get some project experience. I'd met with the team several times already as it was and every time I felt useless and inadequate. Because of my inexperience I didn't have much to offer, so I'd sat through those meetings like a rock, silent and with no purpose.

Then there were my college classes to consider; the courses were interesting and I was learning a lot, but it'd been years since I'd done homework and after years of not studying I was out of practice and I had to work harder on my lessons than I ever had before. In the evenings I fought exhaustion from working all day as I sat at the kitchen table studying instead of relaxing at The Starlight with Josh or nibbling on Lauren's neck as her hands worked their magic on my body. And yet I didn't want to be with Lauren, and playing pool with Josh just didn't seem so interesting to me suddenly.

No—nothing in my life felt right. And then I thought about Harry, thinking, He'd probably understand how I feel. I hated to bother him, but on the other hand, I figured he might have some useful advice for me. It wasn't just me that I was worried about, either; I didn't want to hurt Lauren or Sabrina, I didn't want to mess up my classes, and I didn't want to embarrass Jim by being a total loser on the project team. As it was, though, even my friendship with my best friend was suffering.

I picked up the phone and called Harry's office.

"Want to grab a hamburger at The Viking?" Harry asked later that day when I stopped by his office to see him after work. "Ann has her girl's night out tonight so I'm batching it."

We walked across the street to The Viking, a tavern known for the biggest and best burgers in town. We grabbed a booth and promptly ordered a basket of onion rings for an appetizer, cheeseburgers, and a pitcher of beer. Once we'd ordered I felt awkward and regretted calling Harry. After all, I wondered, what am I going to say? That I'm a twenty-five-year-old guy who feels lost and confused? That I don't fit in anywhere in my old life or current life? But in the usual Harry style, he immediately put me at ease and soon I was telling him all about my out-of-sorts feelings.

"Nothing feels right," I finished, and took a bite of an onion ring.

"That's because everything's new," he said. "New classes, new work assignments, and a new girlfriend; change isn't easy, kiddo. It isn't comfortable. If it were, people wouldn't be stuck in bad habits and life ruts forever." He topped off my glass of beer from the pitcher on the table and asked, "Do you believe you're headed in the right direction—that the things you're doing are what you want in life?"

I shrugged, hedging a little from uncertainty. "I think so. I like the classes and it's interesting to watch the project team at work, even if I don't have anything to contribute."

"But you will, in time. And Sabrina?"

"I like her," I said, blushing. "A lot." I met his gaze across the table. "She's so different from the other girls I've dated; I've never felt like this before." I laughed softly. "Before, I never thought about marriage and kids, but with Sabrina, suddenly I can see those things— really envision them for myself. But then I get scared, thinking that way."

Harry nodded. "Because it's a change. One of the best ways to get through change is to let others know your concerns."

I snorted. "My buddy, Josh, thinks I'm crazy and Lauren wants the old me back. I'm not sure that telling others is going to help."

"I meant talking to the project team and Sabrina." He smiled when I gave him a horrified look. "For example, with the project team, offer your help."

"But I don't know how to help them."

"Do they know that you even want to help?"

How could they not? I thought. But then I realized that maybe they didn't. They'd never worked with me before, after all, and since I was always so quiet in the meetings, I could suddenly see how they might think that I was just a lackadaisical slacker riding on other people's coattails.

"As for Sabrina—tell her how you feel, kiddo." Harry continued before I could protest, "I learned years ago that expressing your fears in personal relationships really helps."

I gave him a skeptical look. "Really?"

He nodded. "When Ann was pregnant with our first child I was scared to death. I'd never been around babies or children before and while I knew that Ann would be a great mother, I wasn't so sure that I would be a good father. And so, the first few months of Ann's pregnancy I worried in painful silence. She bought baby clothes, talked to her girlfriends, and decorated the spare bedroom, turning it into a nursery while I was tense with self-doubt and worry. Then one night, she was showing me the latest baby things she'd bought and I simply couldn't take it anymore. So I told her my fears and come to find out—she was just as insecure as I was. She'd never changed a diaper; she'd never dealt with a crying baby. She felt totally unprepared to care for an infant, just as I did. But during the months that followed we gave each other strength and understanding as we faced the new experiences of parenthood together."

By the time we'd finished our burgers I felt more resolved about what I had to do. The next day as I sat in a project team meeting I thought about Harry's advice. Initially it sounded so reasonable to me, but suddenly, the idea of offering my assistance when I didn't know how to help sounded weak and whiny. So, as usual, I sat quietly, took notes, and listened as the rest of the team talked about strategies and plans, fully feeling like I had absolutely nothing to contribute. When the meeting finally broke up and everyone filed out of the conference room I felt even worse than before. Harry's advice was of no use to me and I'd spent yet another meeting in silence, feeling like a fifth wheel.

Brian, the team leader, stayed behind the rest of the group to gather his papers and remove a large project chart from the wall. I started to follow everyone out of the room, but the project chart on the wall caught my eye.

"I'll take down the chart for you," I offered.

Brian smiled. "Thanks. Actually, I almost forgot it. I left it in a conference room last week and then I couldn't remember where I left it; I spent half the day retracing my steps until I finally located it."

"I'm glad I'm able to help even a little bit," I said as I rolled up the chart and slipped a rubber band around the tube I'd formed. "Your team is so experienced that it's hard for me to know where to offer my help."

Brian rested his hip on the conference room table and his hands on his knees. "My group has worked together for so long now that I worry that we make it difficult for new members to break in. Everyone just starts talking and before I know it, the meeting's over and new members haven't been able to fit a word in edgewise."

I shrugged. "I'm afraid I don't have a lot to add right now; I'm not very experienced and—"

"That's why Jim assigned you to the team—for you to become more experienced. How are you with Excel spreadsheets and graphs?"

"I've worked with Excel quite a bit, actually."

He stood up and flipped open his briefcase on the conference room table. "Maybe you can help with these, then."

He opened a folder and laid several handwritten pages of numbers on the table. As he explained what he needed, my heart lightened and a feeling of unexpected camaraderie filled my bones. What Brian was describing to me was something that I actually knew I could do. A few minutes later we walked out of the conference room together talking about my classes and some of the programming I'd done.

I felt pleased about the project team when I sat down at my desk—until my phone rang. It was Lauren. She knew that I didn't have classes that night and she wanted to go to The Starlight with Mindy and Josh. Immediately, I wanted to talk to her about our relationship, but I didn't plan on doing it that night—especially not at The Starlight with Josh and Mindy for company and the house band playing so loudly that I'd have to yell to be heard.

"I'll stop over around eight," I told her. We usually got to The Starlight around nine or after, so I figured I'd get to her place early so we could talk.

She immediately misunderstood why I was coming early. "Sounds like you're feeling better." Her voice shifted into a smooth-and-sexy tone that usually made me wish that I were with her at that very moment.

"Yeah; I thought we'd talk and—"

"Talk? Is that what you call it now?" She chuckled. "I'll see you at eight . . . but we won't be talking for long."

Great, I thought as I hung up. Just great. I wasn't looking forward to having that conversation with Lauren in the first place, but knowing that she'd be in a romantic mood when I broached the subject made the unpleasant chore ahead of me even more dreaded.

That night Lauren met me at her door wearing her tightest pair of Seven jeans and a blouse that dipped so low that I didn't have to look twice to see that she wasn't wearing a bra. As soon as I saw her my hormones kicked into overdrive; the weeks I'd gone without sex due to my recovery suddenly felt like years.

"How about a drink?"

She didn't wait for an answer, but walked into the kitchen where she had two mugs chilling in the freezer. She pulled out two beers, popped the tops, and filled the frosty mugs. She handed me one and stepped close to me, letting the fragrance of her sultry perfume tease my senses and rev up my engine. It look every ounce of resistance I possessed for me not to step back and not sweep her into my arms, kiss her mouth thoroughly, and slip off her blouse.

"We need to talk." I tried to sound light, but even to me, my voice sounded forced and pained.

She giggled. "That's right; you said on the phone that you wanted to talk." She winked and started down the hallway to her bedroom.

"Let's sit in the living room, actually." I turned away from her and walked into the living room, where I sat down in a corner of the sofa.

She gave me a quizzical look and sat down on the edge of the sofa next to me. "This isn't about your dream again, is it?"

"Actually, I want to talk about us," I began.

"You don't want to go out with me anymore." Her voice was flat as she edged away from me, putting several feet between us on the sofa. "I can feel it; things haven't been the same between us since the accident."

"I'm not sure we want the same things in a relationship, Lauren," I said as gently as I could. Her hands wrapped around her glass of beer and her eyes were transfixed on the amber liquid in the glass rather than looking at me. "I think I'm ready to have a serious relationship and I don't think that's what you want." Ironically, in the past, girls always broke up with me because they wanted a serious relationship when I didn't.

She lifted her gaze from her glass and her eyes met mine. "Like marriage and kids?"

I nodded.

A small sigh escaped her lips. "I told you months ago how I feel. I just want to enjoy my life right now; I don't want to worry about a husband, kids, and stuff like that—maybe someday, but not for a long, long time." She took a sip of her beer. "Why the sudden change of heart? Is it because of that dream?"

I avoided the touchy subject of the dream and instead spoke of something I could explain. "It's what I saw with Harry and his family. Before, I never understood how much a family could mean to a person."

"There are no guarantees with families," she said. She went on to talk about her brother, who'd had more bouts of trouble with the law than even she could remember. As it was, he only talked to her when he needed money or her help. "What you saw in the hospital is a family on their very best behavior, Joe. It was fairytale stuff—idealistic."

I realized she was probably right about everyone being on their best behavior in the hospital when Harry was so sick, but still—deep down in my heart I knew it wasn't just fairytale stuff. Harry had told me all about how he'd worked over the years to make his marriage successful and how he'd always stood by his sons during times of trouble. I also knew that just because people are related doesn't mean that they have happy relationships with each other; my mother and I were a good example—we had a fractured relationship and would probably never have closeness. No, there weren't any guarantees with relationships and families, but I still wanted to try.

With someone like Sabrina.

Sunday night as I drove to Sabrina's for lasagna I was still thinking about breaking up with Lauren. Even though Lauren and I agreed that we wanted different outcomes in a relationship, I still felt bad about breaking up with her. I realized that she gave me warnings about families and relationships not only because she wanted me to know all the dangers, but also because her own heart was so hurt by those very same things.

When I told Josh about breaking up with Lauren he thought I'd acted too quickly. "You've only been out with Sabrina once," he said. "Maybe after the second date you won't be so crazy about her."

I doubted that my feelings would change, but even if they did, I knew that I'd simply outgrown relationships like the one I had with Lauren.

"Anyway, you sound a little more sure of yourself," Josh had said as we sat in our shared cubicle and talked.

"I still feel out-of-sorts," I admitted, shrugging, "but I'm happy with the changes I'm making. It's just that making changes isn't easy."

He stood up to leave for a meeting with Jim, but hesitated by my chair and put his hand on my shoulder. "You may have changed, but I still want to be your buddy, dude. I hope you know that."

"Always," I responded.

Driving to Sabrina's, I smiled as I remembered the kindness in his eyes, thinking, I'm really lucky to have a friend like Josh.

"This is Matthew," Sabrina said when I arrived and she introduced me to her uncle. He was just leaving her apartment when I got there—a short, gray-haired guy with glasses—and he smiled and shook my hand. I chuckled to myself as I remembered thinking of Matthew as George Clooney.

"You kids have a nice dinner." He gave a little wave and walked out the door. Although he was smiling, there was a wistfulness and longing in his face and voice that he couldn't hide. I quickly mouthed to Sabrina that he was more than welcome to stay and instantly, her face broke out in a smile.

"There's plenty of lasagna if you'd like to stay, Uncle Matthew," she called to him.

He turned and trod back to where Sabrina and I both stood in the doorway with a big smile on his face. "Sure smells good, I must say. . . ."

"I've even got a bottle of Italian red wine." I pulled the bottle from its gift bag and held it out for his approval.

Uncle Matthew pointed to the label with one thin finger and his eyes lit up. "That's a good wine."

I grinned. "Let's open it right away."

"That was so sweet of you to want Uncle Matthew to stay for dinner," Sabrina said. Matthew had just left for home and we were sitting side by side on her sofa. I was enjoying the warmth of her thigh resting against mine and basking in the joys of the evening. The lasagna was the best I ever had, Uncle Matthew's company had made for great conversation, and Sabrina had stolen my heart without even trying. Still, my feeling of wellbeing slowly faded as I thought about the conversation ahead of me.

"Uncle Matthew really likes you, you know." She turned toward me and gave me one of those smiles that reached my toes and made me want to wrap my arms around her forever.

I reached over and took her hand in mine. It was silky soft, warm, and infinitely comforting. We interlocked fingers and her gaze met mine. "Meeting new people and making new friends are the positive outcomes of my accident," I told her. "Because of it, I got to know you."

She nodded and smiled.

I broke our eye contact as I struggled for the right words. I squeezed her hand and glanced back at her, meeting her violet eyes. "I like you, very much," I began.

"I like you, too," she said softly.

"But I'm honestly worried about having a relationship with anyone right now," I said. "Since the accident, I've been trying to figure out what I want in life, and I'm still working on that."

24

"I think you're doing a great job," she said, gently squeezing my hand. "You're taking classes, doing new things at work—"

"But I'm still not comfortable with the new me," I said. "And the last thing I want to do is hurt you while I try to figure myself out."

"I don't want either of us to get hurt," she said. "I've been too busy for serious relationships until now; I think you're the kind of man I want in my life, but I'm honestly still not sure, Joe."

I gave her hand a soft squeeze. "Let's take it slow, then; we won't rush into anything."

She smiled and squeezed my hand back. "That sounds good to me."

I slipped my arm around her shoulders and pulled her close. I rested my cheek on the top of her head, inhaling the sweet perfume of her hair. Right then, she felt so right in my arms.

Right then, my whole life felt right.

While Sabrina and I both agreed that taking our time was the best plan of action for us, we had a hard time staying away from each other after that night. Simply put, we like being with each other too much—having dinners, going to movies, and spending time with Matthew—and as time passed I felt more comfortable in my new roles and more confident about my choices. Confident enough that after six months I presented Sabrina with an engagement ring that she immediately slipped on her finger.

Shortly after we got engaged I was promoted into a consulting job and I am now a permanent member of Brian's team. Josh and I still shoot pool and see each other at work. My friendship with Harry has deepened and we have dinner once a month at The Viking on Ann's girl's night out.

I'll never know for sure where my dream came from. All I know is that I'm glad I paid attention to it and took steps to make my life more meaningful in every way.

THE END

A Novella Visit From Beyond
THE PRESENCE
Finding unexpected helps from unusual places.

My heartbeat quickened as John turned into the driveway leading to the attached garage. He cut the engine, stepped out, and came around to open my door. "Here we are, Karen," he said with a smile. "Welcome home."

I felt a ripple of excitement as I got out of the car for my first glimpse of the house I would share with my husband and his eight-year-old daughter, Alicia. Still reeling from our whirlwind courtship, I was eager to begin my new life with the man I loved. The two-storey structure was white with black shutters. My eyes were drawn to the red and white petunias greeting me from the second storey window boxes when I caught a movement in an upstairs window. The curtains slightly parted and I thought I saw the silhouette of a figure.

"Who is that?" I asked. I'd no sooner spoken before the curtains closed and the figure vanished.

John followed my gaze with a puzzled look. "Who?"

"I thought I just saw someone upstairs."

John shook his head. "I don't think so, honey. Nobody's home."

The scarlet, setting sun sparkled in the windows. Had I only thought I'd seen something? Still, I felt a sudden shiver down my spine. Don't start imaging things, I silently scolded.

"Well, how do you like it?" John asked, opening the trunk to get our luggage.

My momentary uneasiness quickly vanished as I stood admiring my new home. How different life would be here in this small-town setting after living in a big city all my life. The April air was sweet with the fragrance of flowers. The apple tree gracing the front lawn was heavy with pink blossoms. Smiling, I took in the ornate gingerbread trim and sprawling porch with a swing. Crimson potted geraniums on either side of the front door offered a cheery welcome. Surely, I'd seen only a reflection in the upstairs window, I decided as my eyes swept over the Victorian dwelling with its cupola and dormers.

As we climbed the front steps, a sudden breeze rustled through the oak tree on the side of the house and I turned to watch the swaying branches. The sharp caw of a crow on a top limb made the hairs on the back of my neck prickle. Looking back, I sometimes wonder if the

26

fluttering leaves were whispering a wordless warning that something ominous lurked beyond the threshold.

"Oh, John," I said. "It's lovely."

My husband gave me the irresistible smile that captured my heart when we'd first met just weeks ago. "So are you, Karen," he said, leaning over to give me a quick kiss before lifting our suitcases. "I hope life in a small town like Middletown won't be too humdrum for you," he added as I followed him up the front walk.

John had already explained that the houses on our tree-lined street were scattered with numerous vacant lots separating them. Our closest neighbors were two sisters who lived in the house across the way and Mrs. Damon, a middle-aged widow in the gray house next door. The business center of town was half a mile away.

I smiled reassuringly. "Not when I have you and Alicia," I said. Although I didn't say it, I was secretly grateful for the slower pace. After what I'd endured before I met John, I wasn't quite ready for an active social life. But I wondered about Alicia. "Does she have friends nearby?"

He shook his head. "Not right on our street. But she can ride her bike to visit playmates a few blocks away. And her school isn't far at all. She either rides her bike or walks and even comes home for lunch on nice days."

"I can't wait to meet her," I told him. I was both excited and a bit nervous about meeting my stepdaughter. Would she resent my sudden intrusion into her life? Although I knew I could never take her mother's place, I hoped that we would get off to a good start and in time, I could earn a spot in her heart.

"I'm sure you'll love her as much as I do, honey," he said as we climbed the front stairs. "Alicia is such a delight in so many ways. She loves to read and has a vivid imagination, too," he added, paternal pride clearly audible in his voice.

Lowering our suitcases, John unlocked the front door and turned to lift me into his arms. "Welcome home, Mrs. Ellington," he said as he carried me across the threshold.

From the foyer, I caught a glimpse of the spacious living room with its arched entrance and stone fireplace. "Oh, John," I breathed, eager to see the entire dwelling. "I love it already."

"And I love you," he said, lowering me to the floor to pull me into his arms.

My body molded to his. I wound my fingers through his hair to return his deep, passionate kiss. And that's how my stepdaughter first saw me—locked in her father's arms. When we finally drew apart, I turned to find a small girl watching us with hostile eyes and a sullen mouth. A gasp escaped my throat and my carefree mood vanished at the obvious anger in her pretty face. I felt uneasy that she'd seen our embrace. This wasn't the way I'd planned to meet Alicia. Especially when John had told me his daughter was with Mrs. Damon next door.

John turned to follow my startled gaze and his eyes widened in surprise. "Alicia," he cried, moving toward her with outstretched arms.

Her expression changed in an instant. "Daddy!" With a little cry of delight, she flung herself into his arms. "Oh, Daddy, I missed you so much."

"And I missed you, too, angel," he said, stroking her silky hair. He turned in my direction. "This is Karen, honey."

She gave me a stiff smile that didn't reach her eyes. "Hello, Karen," she said in a polite voice. Turning away, she tugged at her father's hand to lead him to the kitchen. "I made supper for you, Daddy," she cooed. "I did it all by myself. Mrs. Damon hardly helped at all."

"That's great, honey," John praised. He ruffled her hair. "But speaking of Mrs. Damon, how come you're not at her house, sweetie?"

"I was," she said, her face proud. "But Mrs. Damon let me come over to set the table. Supper is in her refrigerator. I'll go over and get it."

The rooms were spacious, with high ceilings. I voiced delight in the built-in shelves and charming nooks and crannies that newer houses lacked. Even though it was old, the house had a charm all its own. The kitchen was big enough for a large table with six chairs, and tall windows made the room seem bright and cheerful.

"The laundry room is downstairs," John said as we passed the door leading to the basement. "You can check it out tomorrow, if you like." He added that there were also clotheslines in the yard in case I ever wanted to hang articles outdoors.

At the top of the steep, winding staircase a long hall led to three bedrooms. The first was Alicia's and faced the south. I couldn't resist pausing in the doorway, smiling as I took a quick look. A white bedroom set was graced with a pink floral spread and matching curtains. A collector doll with a china head rested on the ruffled pillow sham. The hutch held miniature dolls, figurines, and books. My heart tugged at the feminine, little girl look of Alicia's room. It reminded me of my own bedroom as a child and I felt a swift bond with my stepdaughter.

The room next to Alicia's was a smaller bedroom that had obviously been used as a sewing room. "What a pleasant room," I said, taking in the white wicker sofa and matching chair. A sewing machine stood in front of the windows. White lace curtains covered the three windows. Looking out, I saw that they faced the west and overlooked the front lawn. I realized, then, that this was the same window where I thought I'd seen someone looking out. Purple and white silk lilacs in a milk glass vase complemented the floral pattern gracing the chintz-covered cushions of the old wicker set.

John's face grew thoughtful. "Lori decorated this room. She loved to sew and made most of Alicia's clothes. Her sewing helped keep her busy when I traveled on business, as well. She spent many happy hours here."

I could sense it in the serenity of the room. Throughout my life, I had felt a distinct atmosphere in some houses. I couldn't explain it other than it was sensitivity or awareness of certain strong emotions like anger, sickness, or love. It didn't happen often but when it did, I later learned that my feelings were accurate. I'd never enjoyed visiting the home of my mother's best friend as a child. It seemed filled with hostility and made me uneasy. When the friend and her husband divorced, my mother was shocked. But not I. I think I knew all along that the woman and her husband hated each other.

Next we went to the master bedroom, where John placed our suitcases on the four-poster bed. Two windows overlooked the front lawn and the third faced north. The bedroom set was cherry wood and quite lovely. The beautifully carved headboard looked antique. The highboy and dresser featured serpentine drawers and brass handle pulls. It was when I ran my fingers admiringly over the soft patina of the wood that I saw the wedding photo. John made a dashing groom standing beside a stunning woman. I could see that Alicia strongly resembled her mother. Both were blessed with large eyes fringed with generous lashes. Although my looks were average, I was certainly not beautiful, like Lori.

"Alicia looks a lot like her mother," I said, lifting the photo. Does John find me plain in comparison to his first wife? I wondered.

Standing behind me, John slid his arms around my waist and looked over my shoulder. "I'm sorry about that photo." His voice sounded troubled. "It's been there ever since Lori and I were married. I should've called Mary and asked her to take it down before we arrived."

"Mary?" I echoed, not knowing whom he meant.

"Mary Damon," he explained. "The neighbor who has been seeing Alicia off to school and taking care of her afterward until I get home. Mary also stayed with Alicia full-time when I had to travel on business."

"It sounds as if Mrs. Damon has been a Godsend after you lost Lori," I said.

He nodded. Taking the frame from me, he quickly opened it and removed the photo of him and Lori. "I'll put this away, Karen," he said with a smile, handing me the empty frame. "Our wedding photo belongs here now."

I bit my lip. "But what about Alicia?" I asked. "Won't she be upset?"

Smiling, he shook his head. "She has a photo of her mother and herself in her own bedroom. Besides, I'll put this photo in our old photo album so Alicia can still see it whenever she wants."

As if on cue, we heard the back door slam. "I'm back, Daddy," Alicia called. "Come see what I made for supper."

Alicia's meal consisted of canned chili, corn chips, and a salad. She served strawberry ice cream for dessert. Although John and I both showered her with compliments, Alicia practically ignored me. Afterward, she led him to his chair and settled into his lap. She told him about the new kittens in her friend's household, the puppy that had wandered into her classroom, and about a new dress Mrs. Damon was making for her. John seemed enchanted with his small daughter and I didn't blame him. It wasn't going to be easy but somehow, in time, I hoped to become a part of their closeness.

I tried to join in their conversation and John did his best to include me, too. But Alicia answered my questions as briefly as possible, turning her attention back to her father. Aware that my efforts were futile, at least for tonight, I finally pasted a smile on my face and excused myself. "Guess I better start unpacking," I said, rising from the sofa.

"Need some help?" John asked.

Before I could answer, Alicia spoke. "But, Daddy," she pleaded, her mouth forming a soft pout, "I want to show you my drawing. And don't you want to see the award I got for winning the spelling bee last week?"

"You bet I do, angel," he said.

"It's up in my room," she explained, climbing off his lap. As they passed to go up the staircase ahead of me, Alicia shot me a triumphant look. "See?" her smug smile seemed to say. "He's still mine!"

While John was with his daughter in her room at the end of the hall, I unpacked our suitcases and put everything away. John had emptied the dresser for my things while he kept the armoire. Smiling, I slipped our wedding photo in the empty frame that had held the photo John removed and put it on the dresser. Then, I showered and slipped into a silver wisp of a nightie that John had not yet seen. Dabbing cologne on my inner wrists and between my breasts, I thought of our honeymoon. Sweet memories flooded me of those heady days we spent at the island resort. We'd strolled along the beach, enjoying the pounding surf and soaring gulls. We smiled as sandpipers scurried to the edge of the water at our approach.

We also spent heavenly days in each other's arms. I sighed, recalling our passionate lovemaking. It had been over a year since John had lost Lori and my husband, Matt, was killed in a fatal auto accident. We were both hurting when we found each other. John had come to St. Louis on an extended business trip and we met at the opening of an art exhibit. The attraction was mutual and strong. We ended up spending every free moment John had together. By the end of his stay, John asked me to marry him and I accepted.

John phoned Mrs. Damon and also spoke with his daughter to tell him of our wedding plans. After my gentle prodding, John reluctantly admitted that Alicia, his eight-year-old daughter, did not sound too happy about it. "She just needs time to get used to the idea," John assured. "I'm sure the two of you will hit it off and she'll love having a wonderful, loving stepmother like you, Karen."

Now, as I got ready for bed, I wasn't so sure. Alicia had been polite but definitely cool and she hadn't been at all friendly this evening. I realized, though, that her father had been her whole world. And his sudden marriage must've upset the child. I'd have to be understanding and patient. Surely, I told myself, Alicia will warm up to me in time. I was determined to work hard at establishing a rapport between us. Glancing at the bedside clock, I saw that it was nearly ten. Late, it seemed, for a child who had to go to school in the morning.

Climbing into bed, I pulled the sheet over me and was nearly asleep when John came in. I opened my eyes to find him smiling, probably at something amusing Alicia had said. I sat up, lowered the sheet, and held out my arms to him. "I've been waiting for you," I said softly.

"Oh, Karen." His voice was husky with emotion. "I love you so much." He unbuttoned his shirt, slipped it off, and dropped it on the floor. His shoes and socks followed the shirt and then slowly, agonizingly, he shed the rest of his clothing. I felt the familiar warmth spread through my body as I took in his lean, muscular body. His eyes filled with hunger, he moved slowly toward me. In moments, his mouth was fastened on mine.

In the heat of his embrace, I forgot everything—my concern about Alicia, the tragedy of my husband's death, and the anguish I'd endured afterward. With my new husband's strong body pressed against mine, I thrilled to the warmth of his mouth raining soft kisses on my neck.

The next morning I awoke to the morning sunlight slanting into the room. With a start, I sat up and glanced at the clock. Seven-thirty! I heard John singing in the shower. I hurried into the bathroom to rinse my face and brush my teeth. I pulled on a rose velvet robe and rushed downstairs to start breakfast.

I found Alicia, already dressed for school, seated at the table. I was surprised to see that a woman stood before the stove, placing scrambled eggs onto a plate.

"Good morning," I greeted. "I'm Karen."

"Pleased to meet you, Karen," the woman said, smiling as she put the eggs in front of Alicia. "I'm Mary Damon. I live next door."

"I've heard a lot of nice things about you, Mary." I smiled and sat down across from Alicia. "I'm sorry I slept so late," I apologized. "I meant to get Alicia's breakfast this morning. I'll do better tomorrow."

"Nothing to be sorry about," Mary said, her eyes twinkling as she poured me a cup of coffee. "John asked me to come over this morning because he knew you'd be tired from the trip and might want to sleep in."

"Thank you, Mary." I glanced at Alicia. She didn't look at me or say anything. Her head was bent over the plate and she concentrated on rearranging the eggs, not eating. "Good morning, Alicia," I said in a bright voice.

"Hi, Karen," she said without enthusiasm. Her eyes met mine briefly before returning to her plate.

Mary broke the awkward silence that followed by telling me that John had also asked her to stock the kitchen cabinets and refrigerator with staples before our arrival. "You can check the freezer in the basement, too," she said, taking a tray of bacon from the microwave. "I have everything wrapped in freezer paper and labeled."

I gave her a grateful smile. "That's great, Mary. No wonder John sings your praises."

"Oh, I'm happy to help." She smiled and her cheeks brightened with pleasure. "Sure is a beautiful morning, isn't it? Listening to the birds chirp when I walked over here told me they think so, too."

I chuckled at her remark and nodded in agreement. "I think our feathered friends know what the day will be like better than weather forecasters do," I said. The sun streamed into the kitchen and I caught the sweetness of honeysuckle as the curtains billowed in a gentle breeze. It smelled heavenly.

When John entered the breakfast area, Alicia ran to him, hugging him fiercely. He picked her up and she wrapped her arms around his neck and whispered into his ear. I tried to smile, waiting for him to tell his daughter not to whisper, that it wasn't polite. Instead, he whispered something back, making her giggle.

When Mrs. Damon put a plate of bacon and eggs on the table for John and me, he sat Alicia down beside him and began to eat. Alicia followed suit.

"This is good," she said, smiling at John. "Everything tastes better when you're sitting next to me, Daddy."

She shifted her gaze to me for a second or two, as if to see if I'd heard her remark. I guess it was only natural that Alicia felt I was competing for her father's love and attention, but I found her behavior rather disturbing. As I lifted my fork, John gave me a long look, his mouth curving into a secret smile. I knew he was remembering last night's lovemaking. So was I. That and the love reflected in his eyes brightened my spirits. Smiling, I reminded myself that my stepdaughter was only eight and I was an adult. If I could just remain patient and understanding, in time she'd warm up to me and no longer resent that I was now a part of her father's life.

When Alicia finished eating, Mrs. Damon asked her if she remembered the homework assignment she had helped her with yesterday. Alicia clapped her hand over her mouth. "Uh oh," she said. "I think I left it in my bedroom. I'll run up and get it right now.

"Thank you for reminding me, Mrs. Damon," she said in a sweet voice when she returned. "May I come to your house after school the way I always do?"

Mrs. Damon hesitated, then glanced at John and me with a questioning look. I lowered my eyes and sipped my coffee. I didn't feel that it was my place to decide.

"Are you sure you don't want to come straight home today?" John asked, looking at me.

Alicia shook her head. "Mrs. Damon said she might finish my new party dress today," she explained. "So I want to be there to try it on."

"Is that all right with you, Mary?" John asked, a disappointed expression on his face.

Mrs. Damon smiled and nodded. "Of course it is," she said with a smile. "Besides, Alicia can try on the dress so I can hem it. That way, she'll have it for her friend's birthday party on Saturday."

Alicia's face lit up. "Maybe we can bake some brownies, too."

Mrs. Damon laughed and tousled her hair. "We'll see, sugar." With a nod at me, Mrs. Damon said good-bye and left through the back door.

I was pleased to see Alicia carry her plate to the sink, for it showed me that she had learned to be helpful. Gathering her backpack and windbreaker, she smiled at John. "Bye, Daddy," she said, giving him a quick hug.

"Have a good day at school, angel," he said.

"Are you coming home for lunch today?" I asked, planning to do my best to fix something special if she was.

She shook her head. "Mrs. Damon already packed me a lunch."

I tried to hide my disappointment with a smile. "Then I guess I'll see you at dinner, Alicia."

She nodded but did not return my smile. "Bye, Karen," she said in a flat voice, heading out the door.

"Before I get going," John said, rising. "I want to show you something."

I followed him to the door leading to the attached garage. John stopped by a wooden key rack hanging to the left of the door. "Here's where we keep all our keys, honey. And these," he said, lifting a set from the hook on the far right, "are the keys to your car."

He opened the door and led me to a white, late-model car parked next to his. "I've kept up the maintenance and driven it periodically, so it's in good shape."

I ran my fingers over the smooth, waxed hood. "Did it belong to Lori?" I asked.

He nodded. "Yes, but it's yours now." Flashing the dimpled smile that always melted my heart, he gave me the keys. "And a full tank of gas, too."

I was happy to have a car of my own, of course, but it gave me an eerie feeling knowing it had first belonged to John's late wife. He hadn't told me the details of her death. All I really knew was that Lori had fallen down the stairs, breaking her neck in the fatal accident. Her sudden death was probably still difficult to discuss so I planned to wait until he was ready to tell me more. I could certainly understand, for I felt the same way about Matt. Even though my husband was killed over a year ago, it wasn't easy to stir up painful memories.

"Maybe I'll take a drive into town today," I said. John had given me a quick rundown of the shops when we drove through the business section yesterday. I also planned to see if any vacant shops might be available. Eventually, I planned to open another consignment shop here in Middletown.

"Good idea," he said, hitting the button to open the electric garage door. "Enjoy yourself today, Karen. And don't worry about dinner, either. If you don't feel like cooking, the three of us will go out to eat tonight."

After John left, I went upstairs to choose an outfit to wear into town. When I moved into the adjoining bath to take a shower, I was surprised to find it didn't have an exhaust fan. But then, I had always enjoyed the conveniences of a modern apartment and remembered that this was an older house.

The warm water felt so good that I stood under the spray longer than usual. When I finally turned off the water and slid back the shower curtain, I saw that the room was hot and steamy. I quickly toweled myself, slipped into my robe, and went into the bedroom to dress. I'd just donned my slacks set when I felt a sudden draft. One window was open a few inches. Perhaps it had turned cool, I thought, closing it. Still, an inexplicable feeling of apprehension rippled through me as I returned to the dresser mirror.

I was applying lipstick when, out of the corner of my eye, I thought I saw movement. I turned to see steam curl out of the open bathroom door. It came in a steady stream to gather in the corner of the room. The steamy mass kept growing and swirling until it seemed to take the form of a figure. My scalp prickled as I watched the spectral image move closer, then dissipate and vanish.

When my heart finally stopped pounding, I grabbed my purse and hurried down the staircase, anxious to leave the house. As I reached for the car keys, my thoughts were whirling. Taking a deep, shaky breath, I tried to comprehend what I'd just seen. When steam from my shower suddenly escaped the bathroom, had I only imagined that it resembled a ghostly shape? Surely, that was it, I tried to tell myself.

Or was it something else? I grasped the doorknob leading to the garage. Feeling vaguely uneasy, I looked over my shoulder. As I entered the garage and headed for the car that once belonged to Lori, an even more disturbing question haunted me. Did something eerie and supernatural lurk within these walls? Was there an unseen presence in the house?

I enjoyed exploring a few interesting shops in town. Most of my time was spent browsing through a specialty shop that carried a wide variety of gift items and antiques. I bought a piece of scrimshaw for John, a Wedgwood plate for myself, and a small porcelain doll for Alicia. By the time I paid for my purchases and headed back to the car, I found myself humming. My earlier uneasiness forgotten, my mood was bright as the sunlit sky. I could hardly wait to give Alicia the doll, and hoped she'd be pleased with her gift. I also hoped she would become the daughter I'd always longed for and yearned to develop a close relationship.

I picked up pastries and a few other items at the supermarket before heading home. As I drove down the tree-lined streets, my thoughts moved backward in time. Matt and I had been so in love. We were high school sweethearts and married two years after graduation. Shortly afterward, my widowed mother died and I used my inheritance to open a resale shop while Matt joined the family business. He managed one of his father's florist shops. Five years later, Matt designed a special device to be used to facilitate the creation of even lovelier floral arrangements. The royalties from his patented invention provided us with a lovely home and many luxuries. The only thing we couldn't seem to have was a family of our own. Still, we were young and kept reassuring each other that we had plenty of time.

But time ran out one fateful evening when Matt and I were on our way to a friend's Christmas party. Our car skidded on an icy patch of road. We spun off the highway and into a ditch. I remember the car flipping over and over until I blacked out. When I came to, I was in the hospital with a broken arm and fractured ribs. My physical pain was nothing compared to my mental anguish when I learned that my beloved husband was dead.

In the months that followed Matt's death, I not only grieved but suffered from guilt feelings, as well. Why had I survived the accident, while Matt was killed? When I sank into a deep depression and suffered emotional problems, I had to be hospitalized. Even when I was released, my psychiatrist still prescribed antidepressants and tranquilizers. I had relied on my manager to take over my shop during my breakdown and was glad to go back to work again. My boutique sold gently used designer clothing and quality jewelry on consignment and business was brisk. I had financial security, as Matt had left me well provided for and I made a good income from my shop. But I never thought I would love again until I met John Ellington.

When he first smiled at me, I felt something stir within me that I thought had died along with Matt. Over a candlelit dinner, we learned that we had both lost our spouses to fatal accidents. Something magical happened that first evening and a whirlwind courtship followed.

When John asked me to marry him, I accepted. Even though friends questioned the wisdom of acting so quickly, I brushed their concerns aside. After selling my business to a frequent patron whom had previously expressed interest in my shop, John and I wed and left on our honeymoon.

Now, as I drove back to the house I shared with my new husband and his daughter, I felt renewed determination to be patient and understanding with Alicia. The child had lost her mother and now she probably thought she was losing her father to another woman. Alicia probably thought I was an interloper planning to take her mother's place. I knew I could never do that. My goal was to win a place in Alicia's heart.

As soon as I got home, I put the gifts I'd bought for John and Alicia in my dresser drawer, and then opened the bedroom windows. The day was warm and the scent of blossoms wafted into the room, the fragrant breeze lifting the curtains. I put my Wedgwood plate in its display rack on the bottom shelf of the built-in wall niche and stood admiring it before making myself a light lunch. I was pleased to see that Mrs. Damon had even made a pitcher of iced tea. I'd just finished eating when the doorbell rang. I opened the door to find two young women standing on the porch, wearing friendly smiles.

"Hi, neighbor," greeted the petite one holding a bouquet of pink peonies. "My sister and I live right across the street. I'm Helen. We came to welcome you to the neighborhood," she said, presenting me with the flowers.

"I'm Julie," said the taller one who carried a covered dish. "And," she added with a wink, "I brought you my world famous chicken casserole."

"Well, thank you," I said, warmed by their friendliness. "And I'm Karen. Please come in."

After placing the casserole in the refrigerator, I found a vase for the flowers. "These are lovely," I said. Helen told me the peonies were from their garden as I served the two sisters iced tea and set out a plate of cookies I'd bought. "I'm so glad to meet you," I said as we sat at the kitchen table.

"To tell you the truth, we could hardly wait," Helen confessed with a dimpled smile. "Ever since Mary told us John got married again, Julie and I have been dying to meet you."

I burst out laughing. "Well, it's good to know I have honest neighbors," I said, delighting in her candor. Helen was pretty with her stylishly cut hair and trim figure.

Julie grinned. "You have to keep in mind that this is a small town, Karen. Getting a new neighbor is a big event here in Middletown."

During our get-acquainted chat, I learned that when Helen, a real estate agent, was divorced, she returned to the old family home to live with her older sister. Julie was a nurse who worked different shifts at the local hospital.

"If you ever need anything, just holler," Helen said. "I just work part-time at the real estate office and show houses on weekends or whenever I get a call. One of us is usually home if you ever need a hand or a sympathetic ear."

Why would I need a sympathetic ear? I wondered. Surely, it was just a figure of speech. Stop looking for hidden meanings, I silently scolded.

"And if you like to jog," Helen added, "let my sister know." She gave Julie a fond glance. "Miss Fitness, here, does her daily laps day or night, no matter what shift she's working."

"No wonder you're so slim," I said, taking in her willowy figure. I explained that I preferred riding a bike and planned to get one.

"So what do you think of Alicia?" Helen asked with an expectant look.

Her question took me by surprise. "Well, I barely met her," I said. "I mean, just for a short time yesterday and this morning." I certainly wasn't about to tell them that I felt that she resented me and risk sounding like the proverbial wicked stepmother!

"Pretty little thing, isn't she?" Julie asked. Her voice sounded wistful. Julie, not as pretty as her sister, had a thin face and plain features. Still, I found that her warm, friendly manner added sparkle to her lackluster appearance.

"She certainly is," I agreed. A lot like her mother, I silently added.

"Sometimes she can be quite a handful," Helen said with a sigh. "But I guess it's to be expected after what happened to her mother."

"Yes, she must miss her so," I said, my heart aching for Alicia's loss. She was so young to know such sorrow.

Julie agreed. "But at least the psychiatrist helped Alicia get rid of her guilt."

"Guilt?" I echoed in confusion, looking from one sister to the other. "I don't understand."

After an awkward pause, Helen spoke. "Surely John told you what happened?"

"Well, yes," I said with a nod. "He said Lori fell down the stairs."

"Yes, she did. The basement stairs," Helen said. "And it was Alicia's fault."

My mouth went dry. "What—what do you mean?"

"It was just an accident," Julie was quick to add. "After all, she was just a little girl. It had been raining for days and that's why Alicia decided to roller skate in the basement. It seems she was carrying her skates down the stairs when Lori called to her from the kitchen."

"She wanted to treat Alicia to hot chocolate and freshly baked cookies," Helen interjected. "Then Alicia's friend phoned to say her mother would drop her off at the house so she and Alicia could play."

She explained that the two children were playing up in Alicia's room when Lori went down the basement stairs carrying a basketful of clothes to wash. She skidded on one of the roller skates Alicia had forgotten and fell down the stairs, landing headfirst on the concrete floor.

"It's so awful," Julie said in a soft voice. "To think that Lori fell to her death slipping on her daughter's forgotten roller skate. Poor Alicia overheard the talk and felt as if she had killed her mother. But it wasn't really her fault. It was just a tragic accident."

The news took me by surprise. It also gave me a greater understanding of Alicia's behavior. The poor child not only lost her mother but felt responsible for her death. No wonder she needed to see a psychiatrist. Just as I had needed help to recover from my guilt over surviving the accident that killed Matt. Even though I'd stopped taking my medications, I still kept a full bottle of tranquilizers in my dresser drawer.

"Does Alicia ever talk about her mother's death?" I wondered aloud.

"Not that I know of," Julie said. "Of course, she may discuss it at times with her father."

"But she used to act out her feelings," Helen added. She explained that Alicia often had temper tantrums and broke things. "Poor Mary went through a lot with her for a while. She even smashed one of Mary's treasured teacups from a set that belonged to her mother."

"Does she still do that?" I asked, feeling uneasy.

"Not that I know of," Julie said. "We didn't mean to upset you, Karen."

"And you haven't," I defended with a laugh. "I guess I just asked because I purchased an expensive Wedgwood plate this morning and put it on the living room shelf."

They both gave me reassuring smiles and made it clear that Alicia hadn't had an outburst in a long time. "You don't have to worry about anything like that, Karen," Helen said. "Alicia seems to be just fine now."

"Still, I'm glad you told me," I said. "I'm sure it will help me understand Alicia. I do want to get close to her." I flashed a grateful smile. "Would you like to see the gift I bought her this morning?" I added that I planned to wrap it before Alicia came home from Mary's house in the afternoon. "I hid it in our bedroom," I added, as they followed me up the stairs.

When I showed them the antique doll, both were enthusiastic. "May I hold it for a closer look?" Helen asked, placing her small shoulder bag on the dresser before I gave the doll to her. "Oh, it's adorable," she cooed, admiring the painted face. "Alicia will love it."

"She sure will," Julie agreed. "What a sweet thing to do, Karen."

"I've always wanted a daughter," I admitted, pleased that they liked the doll. They also liked John's gift. As we left the room, Julie hesitated and told us to go downstairs without her. "I'll be down in a minute," she said with an apologetic smile, heading for the bathroom. "Suddenly, I have to powder my nose."

I took the two gifts with me and Helen and I went downstairs. They were both wrapped in the pastel tissue paper I'd bought at the supermarket by the time Julie joined us in the kitchen. As the sisters went to the door, they urged me to stop by whenever I liked, that I was always a welcome guest. Suddenly, Helen stopped in her tracks. "Oops," she said. "I forgot my purse. I'll run upstairs and get it."

Julie and I made small talk until she returned. Breathing in the sweetness of the peonies, I told her how I loved their smell. "I also love the heavenly smell of lily of the valley."

Julie lifted her brows and tilted her head. "Really? That was Lori's favorite, too. In fact, that's the only cologne she ever used."

"Good thing I remembered my purse," Helen said in a breathless voice. "The keys are in it and I have to open the real estate office tomorrow morning." Smiling, she added, "By the way, Karen, I just love your red blouse. Is it silk?" When I nodded, she said she, too, loved silk but hated to pay dry cleaning bills.

"This is the new kind of silk that's hand washable," I explained. "I just rinse it in cold water and hang it up to drip dry."

"Hey, that's great," she said. She and Julie agreed that something silk would soon be in their wardrobes.

"Thanks again for the flowers and casserole," I added, giving them a friendly wave as they headed across the street.

I spent the rest of the afternoon taking inventory of the kitchen and touring the downstairs in greater detail. John had given me free rein to redecorate if I wanted to make changes. Then I went outside to explore the property and the backyard. I was admiring the scarlet roses climbing the trellis beside the back door when I heard a cheerful greeting. "Hello there, Karen."

I turned to see Alicia and Mrs. Damon coming from her house to ours, carrying an aqua dress on a hanger. "I see you finished Alicia's party dress," I said. "It sure is pretty." I gestured at the trellis. "So are these roses," I added. "I was just admiring them."

"Those are Mommy's roses," Alicia said, giving me a proud smile. "She planted them when I was a little girl and that's why they're my favorite flowers in the whole garden."

"I think they'll be my favorite, too," I said, smiling at her delightful remark. Alicia was still a little girl as far as I was concerned.

Once we went inside, Mrs. Damon beamed as I complimented the dress. "I'll just go hang it in your closet, Alicia, dear," she said, climbing the staircase while Alicia went into the living room to watch television. When Mrs. Damon returned, I told her about my visit with Helen and Julie and showed her the peonies.

"They're good neighbors," Mrs. Damon said. "Julie was such a help when John's mother was dying." She explained that when John's mother was diagnosed with terminal cancer, John insisted that she come to live with him. Lori couldn't look after the old woman, of course. She had her hands full with Alicia and working part-time, so Julie took a leave of absence to look after John's mother. "She was wonderful and even arranged for hospice care near the end. You just ask John, Karen. He can't say enough nice things about good-hearted Julie."

John confirmed Mrs. Damon's story later, when Alicia was upstairs trying on her new dress for us. "I'll always be grateful to Julie. Thanks to her, my mother never felt alone and was spared needless suffering. She's quite a woman."

After Alicia modeled her new dress, she quickly changed and we went out to dinner. I felt encouraged by Alicia's good spirits and pleasant manner at the restaurant. When we got home, I gave her the

40

antique doll. Her face lit up when she saw it. "Oh, she's pretty. Thank you, Karen," she said, giving me a sweet smile.

While Alicia got ready for bed, I gave John his gift and he seemed pleased. "I'm so lucky to have found you, Karen," he said, pulling me close.

I was in high spirits the rest of the evening—until we went upstairs. That's when I found our wedding photo face down on the dresser. I lifted it to find the glass shattered like a giant web. What is going on in this house? I wondered.

Hearing my gasp at seeing the shattered glass, John poked his head out of the walk-in closet. "What's wrong?" he asked.

"Look!" I said in a choked voice.

He hurried to my side. "The picture must've fallen over," he said.

"But how?"

"The windows are open," he noted. "Maybe a sudden breeze knocked it over."

"Or maybe someone broke it," I blurted. As soon as the words were spoken, I regretted them.

He gave me an angry look. "You mean Alicia? You're not being fair, Karen," he said in a tight voice. "She wouldn't do something like this."

I bit my lip. "Are you sure?" I wasn't. Not after what I'd learned today.

"I'm positive," he said tersely. "Subject closed, okay?"

Tears stung my eyes at his tone. When we went to bed, he turned his back and moved to the far side of the bed. Our first quarrel, I thought, feeling miserable. I lay awake, my thoughts churning until I finally fell asleep.

Knowing John would defend his daughter, I let the matter drop. When other incidents occurred, I didn't dare voice my suspicions. Not even when I found a crack zig-zagging down my Wedgwood plate. Surely, that hadn't fallen. It was still on the shelf. Was Alicia acting out her resentment of me? Things got worse about a week later. It was Alicia who made the discovery that awful morning when she left for school. Most of the beautiful scarlet roses Lori had planted had been cut and strewn about the base of the trellis.

When I heard her scream, I ran outside and gasped in dismay. "Oh, Alicia," I cried, rushing to her side. "Your mother's roses! Who could've done such a cruel thing?"

Cradling a withered flower in her small hands, she just stared at me with accusing eyes, tears streaming down her cheeks. Her lips trembling, she turned and ran. "Alicia," I called, but she didn't respond. My heart sank as I watched her head for school with her small shoulders slumped in misery.

Alicia showed her father the rose trellis when he came home and he did his best to comfort her. "I can't imagine who did this, angel," he said, stroking her hair. "But the roses should grow back."

Later, when it was just the two of us, John said very little, looking preoccupied. When I asked what was wrong, he brought up the rose trellis. "I can't understand it," he said, shaking his head. "It could be a kid's prank, but I don't think any local kids would do something so mean. They're a pretty decent bunch and most of them seem to like Alicia."

I stiffened. "Why don't you just say it?" I asked in a tight voice. He gave me a puzzled look. "Say what?"

"You think I destroyed the roses. Alicia convinced you I'm to blame, didn't she?" Once I'd spoken, I realized how I sounded. Emotionally distraught and out of control. Is it happening again? I agonized, my mouth suddenly dry as parchment. Is stress pushing me toward another emotional breakdown? Tears stinging my eyes, I fled the room.

The next day, Helen came over when she saw me in the yard. "I heard about the roses," she said. "Alicia told Mary about it, and Mary told Julie and me."

I bit my lip. "Did Alicia also tell her she thinks I did it?"

Helen gave me an apologetic look. "Maybe she does. But we both know you had nothing to do with it, Karen."

"Thanks," I said, grateful for her faith in me. "No, I didn't, Helen. And I can't imagine who did."

She shuffled her feet, looking uncomfortable. "I may as well come right and say it," she said with a sigh. "Isn't it possible that Alicia cut the roses herself?"

My jaw went slack. "But why? It doesn't make sense."

Her smile was rueful. "Doesn't it? Who would be the most likely suspect, Karen? You would, right? Maybe Alicia did it to cause trouble between you and John."

Her words echoed in my mind the rest of the day, but it seemed so preposterous that I wasn't sure what to think. That evening, John assured me nobody suspected me of vandalizing the roses and nothing more was said about the incident. Still, my nerves were on edge. I felt tense and jumpy, as if waiting for the other shoe to drop.

Two days later, I received a letter from my friend, Tracy, back in St. Louis. She asked how things were going. I'm sure your emotional problems are behind you for good, Karen, she wrote. She went on to say that she admired me for getting help and being hospitalized when I needed it.

When I answered Tracy, I didn't mention any of the problems I was having. I wrote a cheerful letter assuring her that everything was fine. I placed the letter in the mailbox near the curb and lifted the flag. Even if we didn't get mail, the carrier would know we had outgoing mail to be picked up.

Much as I tried, I couldn't stop thinking about the roses. Then, when I went shopping the following week, I heard something that made me feel even worse. I was browsing the magazine rack at the variety store in town when I overheard a conversation in the next aisle. I tensed when I realized the two women were talking about me.

"Have you seen John Ellington's new wife yet?" a woman asked.

I heard a derisive laugh. "Karen? I saw her shopping in the supermarket the other day. She sure can't hold a candle to Lori, can she?"

"Too bad he didn't keep seeing Helen," she said. "John should've married a local girl instead of an outsider."

Her friend agreed. "I wonder what John sees in her?"

"Money," her friend replied. "I hear she's got plenty."

Tears stung my eyes. I quickly returned the magazine to the rack and hurried out. Surely, it isn't true. John loves me as much as I love him, I told myself. Doesn't he?

When I pulled into the driveway, Mrs. Damon came out of her house and waved. "Lovely day, isn't it?" she chirped, heading toward me with a covered dish. "I baked cookies today, so thought I'd bring some over for Alicia."

I pasted a smile on my face, but my voice sounded strained as I thanked her.

"Are you all right, Karen?" she asked, concern reflected in her eyes.

"I'm fine," I lied. "Just a little tired, that's all."

When I mentioned the conversation I'd overheard to Helen and Julie the next day, I left out the part about John marrying me for my money. I just told them I was compared unflatteringly to Lori.

"Some of the woman around here are notorious gossips," Julie assured, patting my hand. "Believe me, Karen, those kinds of women look for the worst in everyone."

I turned to Helen with a stiff smile. "They also said you and John dated for a while."

Helen laughed. "I hardly call having dinner together a few times dating. Especially when all we did was cry on each other's shoulders." She explained that John was dejected about losing Lori and she was upset about her divorce. "Misery loves company, you know. There was nothing romantic between us, Karen, and we both went our separate ways soon afterward."

"She's right," Julie agreed. "Don't let what busybodies said bother you."

But it did. The conversation I'd overheard sent my imagination into overdrive. What if what they said about John marrying me for my money was true? Could he be responsible for all the frightening incidents? John knew of my past emotional problems. Was he trying to drive me to having another breakdown so he could have me committed? That way, he could gain control of my assets. My thoughts churning, I remembered how friends had warned me that I was rushing into marriage with a man I hardly knew.

A couple of weeks later, I discovered most of the pansies I'd recently planted on the side of the house uprooted and strewn about. My hands flew to my mouth as I surveyed the damage. Did Alicia do this in retaliation for the roses?

Mrs. Damon was out hanging clothes and came over. "Oh, what a shame, Karen," she said, her face lined with sympathy. "I'll bet it a dog dug them up." She added that some dogs in the area were allowed to roam free and occasionally wandered into yards. "One of the dogs, I hear, is quite a digger."

"That must be what happened," I said, forcing a smile. But I didn't think it was a dog at all! Was it my stepdaughter lashing back at me? Or was John trying to drive me over the edge?

Even doing laundry made me uneasy. Every time I went down the basement stairs, I thought of Lori falling to her death. The atmosphere seemed so charged with negativity, I was always anxious to finish my task and leave.

One Saturday, while Alicia was riding her bike, I went outside to get my red silk blouse that I'd hung to drip dry earlier. When I found it cut to shreds, flapping in the breeze, an anguished cry escaped my throat. With trembling fingers, I took the ravaged blouse from the line. Icy fingers touched my spine. Someone, I felt certain, hated me! Who did this? I agonized. Was it Alicia—or Mrs. Damon? I saw her leave in her car just minutes ago. Was she secretly tormenting me? Was she upset about the baby-sitting job she lost because I married John? Unanswered questions whirled through my mind like a kaleidoscope of confusion.

One morning, I was upstairs putting away clean towels in the linen closet and detected a floral fragrance. When it grew stronger, I realized it was the scent of lily of the valley. Julie's words returned to haunt me. Lily of the valley, she'd said, was the only cologne Lori ever used. Suddenly, I shivered and felt icy prickles down my back as I became aware of a presence. My heart thudding, I felt as if the spirit of Lori hovered around me. I sensed a strong emotion in the air. Anger? What did Lori want? Was she trying to drive me away? Or was it something else? Maybe, the thought flashed through my mind, Lori is trying to tell me something!

Closing the linen closet door with a bang, I hurried down the hall and quickly descended the staircase. When I reached the kitchen, with its open window, I stood trying to catch my breath. By the time I could breathe normally again, the ghostly fragrance was gone. Maybe I'd only imagined everything, I tried to tell myself.

My growing anxiety began to take its toll and I began having accidents. Like when I decided to repaint the den. I washed it down the first day and left the ladder up. When I climbed it the next day, I heard a cracking sound. The second rung from the top suddenly split in half and I toppled to the floor. The fall knocked the wind out of me. When I finally struggled to my feet, my legs felt shaky and my head thudded. Nothing seemed broken but I was bruised and sore for several days. When I told John, he seemed concerned and went out to buy a new ladder.

When Julie asked about my bruises, I told her about the accident. "You seem so unstrung lately, Karen," she said, looking worried. "It's certainly understandable with all that's happened. Just be careful, okay? And don't forget, if you ever need someone to talk to, I'm here for you."

"Thanks, Julie," I said. "I can see why John sings your praises." I was surprised to see her blush at my compliment.

A few days later, I got an electrical shock when I plugged in my hair dryer. I quickly dropped it and pulled the plug. That's when I saw the frayed cord and exposed wires. It didn't make sense, because the hair dryer was practically new.

I grew even more distressed when I found myself misplacing items. One day, I couldn't find the iron until I opened the refrigerator and found it on the bottom shelf. I was sure I hadn't put it there! Household items were not only moved, but missing. Sometimes, after I shopped for groceries, things would mysteriously disappear from my cupboards. Like the time I was certain I'd bought a can of coffee but the next morning, it was gone. John left for work unhappy that he went without the two cups he so enjoyed. I searched my purse for the store receipt but that was missing, too. Had I thrown it away?

I was plagued with apprehension and doubt. At times, I was convinced that someone was tormenting me and there were also times I feared I was losing my mind. I was riddled with uncertainty the day I placed a roast in the crock pot and set the automatic timer before taking in an early matinee movie. I asked Mrs. Damon to keep an eye out for Alicia after school, hoping the comedy would lighten my mood. When I came home and set the table for dinner, I felt better than I had in weeks. Until I opened the crock pot top and found it cold. The roast looked as raw as when I'd put it in. Lightheaded, I lowered myself into a chair. Had I only thought I set the timer? I whimpered with confusion. I glanced at the clock, aware that John would soon be home. My heart thudding, I quickly backed my car out the driveway and drove to town to buy a prepared chicken dinner.

When John found the roast in the garbage that evening, he gave me a puzzled look. Stammering, I told him that the roast looked like it had gone bad so I discarded it. I found that I was hiding more and more from my husband. I wasn't sure whom I could trust. I didn't know who was responsible for what was happening to me. Was it Alicia or John? Or was it someone else? Even more frightening, I harbored another fear. Was I losing my mind?

My nerves taut, I had difficulty sleeping. Exhausted, I began taking a tranquilizer at bedtime. Just one capsule calmed my nerves and helped me get a good night's sleep instead of tossing restlessly. I felt more rested and when a calm period went by with nothing unusual or frightening occurred, I grew more relaxed. Things finally seemed to be going more smoothly. Filled with renewed hope, I made up my mind to be especially kind and patient to Alicia and really try to make her like me.

I was encouraged when Alicia slowly responded to my overtures. She smiled more and began to include me in conversations with her father. Was she really coming around? I wondered. Or was her behavior just a trick to avert suspicion and throw me off guard? Now that I could think more calmly, I rejected that idea. The more I thought about the bizarre occurrences, the more I doubted that an eight-year-old child could be so devious. I had to admit that what Helen and Julie had told me about Alicia could have affected my judgment. John was right when he said I was being unfair to her. Filled with remorse, I vowed I would make renewed efforts to get closer to my stepdaughter.

I bought myself a bike and went riding with her. I took her shopping one Saturday and afterward, we stopped for lunch. My spirits lifted at the good time we had together. My stepdaughter and I were finally bonding. Alicia began coming home for lunch a few times a week, chatting about school. She showed me her school papers and let me help her with homework. I really began to feel like a mother. When Alicia invited me to her friend's house to see the kittens, I was delighted. One kitten in particular, a black and white female, captured Alicia's heart.

"Can I keep her, Karen?" she asked, her eyes pleading.

"If it's okay with your father," I told her with a smile. "I don't see why not."

Her face lit up and she came over to give me a hug. "Oh, thank you."

When I stopped by to visit Helen and Julie a few days later, I told them how well things were going with Alicia and me. "I'm glad to hear it," Julie said. Was I imagining it or did her smile seem guarded?

When Helen spoke, I understood. "I hope you won't take this the wrong way, Karen, but please don't get your hopes up too high," she cautioned. "And don't let your guard down, either. After all she's been through, Alicia's behavior might still be unpredictable, you know."

Julie sighed. "I didn't want to rain on your parade," she said, nodding in agreement. "But Helen is right. Just be careful."

I knew they meant well, but I tried to brush their warnings aside. Admittedly, Alicia resented me at first, but it was understandable that she felt threatened by an instant stepmother. Pleased that the three of us were on our way to becoming a family, John agreed to let Alicia have the kitten she wanted.

"Kathy's mom says I can come get Checkers in four or five weeks," Alicia said.

"Checkers?" John echoed, with a grin.

Her curls bounced as she nodded her head. "That's what I'm going to call her," she said, her eyes shining as she smiled at us.

The growing bond between Alicia and me brought John and me closer, as well. After we made especially tender love one evening, I finally confided in him and related the strange and frightening things that had been happening. I told John about the accidents, the cracked Wedgwood plate, and the way my pansies and blouse were vandalized. I related how household items are sometimes moved or missing. "I know, now, Alicia had nothing to do with any of it," I said, nestled in his arms. "Still, I don't know what to think."

The only thing I held back was that I sensed something supernatural in the house and felt that the presence of Lori still lingered. "Sometimes," I confessed, "I'm so confused and even wonder it some of it is all in my mind. Oh, John," I asked, in a frightened whisper, "do you think I'm just imagining things?" Relieved that I had finally shared my fears, I began to cry.

"Karen, Karen," he soothed, holding me close until I quieted. His voice tender, he told me that he wished I had told him everything sooner. "I'm convinced something strange is going on all right, honey," he said, stroking my hair. "I'm also certain it's real and you're not imagining it."

Weak with relief, I buried my face in his shoulder. "Oh, John, I've been so afraid. It's such a relief to know you believe me."

"Of course I do." His voice filled with concern. "And I'm worried, Karen. You and Alicia could be in danger. Whoever is behind all this may have a twisted mind. Don't mention anything to anyone else," he warned, his lips brushing my hair. "Not until we find out who's responsible."

"Do you think we should go to the police?" I asked, looking into his eyes.

Frowning, he shook his head. "No," he was quick to reply. "Not yet. At this point, what could they do? I have my suspicions, Karen, but what I need is proof."

"Who do you suspect?" I asked, my thought whirling. "Mrs. Damon?"

He touched a finger to my lips. "I can't say, yet," he told me. "It wouldn't be fair to accuse someone or make you suspect the wrong person. I promise you I'll do all I can to get to the bottom of this. You'll just have to trust me, Karen."

I did trust him—until one frightening morning. I waited until I'd gotten Alicia off to school before taking a shower. When I stepped out of the stall, the room was filled with steam. After drying myself, I reached for my robe hanging on the bathroom door hook. That's when I saw the message on the bathroom mirror. As if a ghostly finger had etched it on the steamy surface, I read the grim warning. A cry of alarm escaped my throat. My eyes widened as I gazed in fearful fascination. The word BEWARE was clearly visible. I watched in terror as the warning slowly dripped, leaving an eerie trail on the surface of the mirror.

My heart thudding, I reached for the doorknob and stumbled out. I sat on the bed until my rapid breathing slowed and my heartbeat returned to normal. While I was getting dressed, a sweet fragrance touched my nostrils. Lily of the valley. I knew, with swift certainty, that Lori had written the message on the mirror. I quickly dressed, my thoughts whirling. What could the message mean? Who should I beware of? I thought of my husband and how he urged me not to call the police. Why? And why had he left Alicia and me, when he claimed to be worried about what was going on? Was Lori trying to warn me that it was John who had been tormenting me?

As I descended the staircase, I heard knocking at the back door. It was Julie in her jogging outfit. Relief flooded through me, as I invited her in. I wouldn't be alone. When she saw my face, her eyes widened. "You look upset, Karen," she said. "Is something wrong?"

The concern reflected in her voice acted as a release and my words suddenly tumbled out. "Oh, Julie," I said, my voice catching. "I'm glad you're here. I'm so afraid."

"Of what?" she asked.

I took a deep breath. "I—I think there's a presence in the house."

She frowned, looking puzzled. "What do you mean?"

I told her about the message on the mirror and the scent of lily of the valley. "I think Lori is trying to warn me," I said. "I think I'm in some kind of danger, Julie." I didn't add that I was afraid the one responsible could very well be John!

"Now, just calm down," Julie said, gently guiding me into a

chair. "You wait here and I'll go upstairs and take a look."

As I waited in the kitchen, I wondered what Julie would find. Was the message still on the mirror? Would she believe me? Or would she think I imagined everything?

When she returned, Julie told me there was absolutely nothing on the mirror. "Why don't I fix you a nice cup of tea?" she asked, going to fill the kettle. "I'm sure Mary left some nice soothing herbal tea in the cupboard. Then we'll talk."

She glanced over her shoulder while she brewed the tea in a teapot, smiling and trying to comfort me in gentle tones. "Drink up, Karen," Julie urged, bringing me a cup of tea. "It will make you feel better. More relaxed."

I did as she said, even though it had an odd taste. I'd never tried the tea until now. As soon as my cup was empty, she took it to the counter to refill it. "Have another cup," she said, joining me at the table.

"Thanks, Julie," I said, lifting my cup. I was starting to feel calmer.

"Talk to me, Karen," Julie said, her voice soothing. "Tell me what's troubling you."

I spoke haltingly at first, and then the words came more easily as I grew more and more relaxed. I repeated all that had been happening in the past weeks, how frightened and confused I'd been. "I've been so afraid."

"Yes, I know you have," she said.

I rubbed my forehead, feeling lightheaded. "I thought it was Alicia."

Julie's eyes glittered and she gave me a strange smile "That's exactly what I wanted you to think."

I frowned. "What—what do you mean?"

"Can't you guess?" She laughed. "Oh, it was all so easy. And Helen helped, too, even though she didn't know it. My sister kept telling you things about Alicia that made you suspect her even more."

I had trouble focusing my eyes as I stared at her. I couldn't believe this was really happening.

"You made it all so easy for me, Karen. Especially with your past emotional problems. You played right into my hands." She laughed crazily. "I found your tranquilizers the day you showed us the doll you bought for Alicia. And I took a letter from your mailbox and steamed it open. That's how I learned you were once hospitalized with an emotional breakdown." She told me how she'd had an extra key made when she'd been taking care of John's dying mother. "I knew whenever you went out, Karen. I watched you from my house. Then I'd go jogging and circle around the back. Mary Damon couldn't see me. Nobody could."

Her face twisted in a bizarre smile, she explained how she had sneaked in with her key to rearrange and take items from the house. "I broke your Wedgwood dish," she admitted. "And cracked your wedding photo. I cut the roses and ruined your flowers. I did it during my off shifts when everyone was sleeping or when Mary Damon was gone from her house. Just as I slashed your blouse. Yes, I did it all, Karen. Oh, you were so easy to fool!"

My mouth went dry and my heart began to thud. "I don't understand," I said, my voice cracking.

Her smile was replaced with a look of hatred. "No, how could you?" she asked, her voice bitter.

I couldn't believe my ears. I blinked several times, trying to focus my eyes as Julie rambled on. "John was the man I'd been waiting for all my life. I knew he was the one who would make up for all my years of loneliness." She looked at me with contempt. "You don't know what it's like to be lonely, to be plain. Neither did Lori. She didn't deserve John. She wouldn't even quit her job to take care of his dying mother. But I did!"

My lightheadedness grew as Julie told me how John kept praising her, telling her how wonderful she was and how he appreciated all she did for his mother. "John was falling in love with me," she said, her eyes wild. "Just as I loved him. I knew I'd make a better wife for John than Lori. That's why I got rid of her."

My lips felt parched. "How?" I asked.

"By pushing her down the basement stairs. Then I put Alicia's skate on the steps so it looked like an accident."

My head spun. "You killed Lori," I gasped. "And let Alicia take the blame!"

"Lori didn't deserve John. And neither do you. He would've asked me to marry him, if you hadn't come along and ruined everything. You stole him from me. Now, you have to die, too!"

My heart thudding, I pushed back my chair. I tried to get up but I felt dizzy. "No, you don't," Julie said, shoving me back into the chair. "You stay right here," she commanded. Reaching into the pockets of her pullover, she withdrew a length of rope and bound my hands behind my back. "With all the tranquilizers I emptied into your tea, it would be dangerous for you to get up, Karen."

Laughing, she told me she'd taken the prescription bottle from my drawer when she went up to check the bathroom. "I emptied the capsules into your tea, Karen. You poor dear. You're so nervous and distraught, you took an overdose."

"You can't get away with this," I said weakly, my heart hammering.

"Can't I?" Her mouth formed a sneer. Her eyes wild, Julie told me how she was going to do it. She would put me in the car and start the engine with the garage door closed. "Everyone knows how nervous you've been lately, Karen. Mary Damon mentioned it and so did my sister. They'll believe that you took tranquilizers before going into the garage to commit suicide."

I struggled to stay alert. How many pills had she dissolved into my tea? How could I stop her? I didn't want to die! "Help!" I yelled.

"Save your breath," Julie said. "Nobody will hear you. Mary Damon left early this morning to visit a friend thirty miles away. She'll be gone all day.

"You're going to be a good girl now," she said in a sing-song voice, yanking me out of the chair. "And get into the car. I'll start the engine and keep your hands tied. I'll wait until you're completely out, dear Karen, before I untie you and leave. Alicia will find you when she comes home from school."

"No," I said, trying to break away. But she had me in an iron grasp as she pushed me toward the garage door. Taking the car keys from the rack on the wall, she shoved me into the garage. My hands still tied behind my back, Julie pushed me into the car and got into the driver's seat. She put the key in the ignition and started the engine.

"It will all be over soon," she said, her eyes wild. "And then John will be mine."

Tears stung my eyes. I thought of John and how wrong I'd been about him and Alicia. I knew I loved my husband and stepdaughter and I didn't want to die. Oh John, I silently agonized, wishing he were here. Help me! Somebody, please help me!

Julie opened the door before pulling me over to the driver's side. "Too bad you can't turn the key with your hands tied behind your back," she taunted, as she got out of the car.

She looked at me with a smirk as she stood beside the car. "I'll check on you in a few minutes," she said. "It won't take long." All at once, my eyes were drawn to the door leading from the garage into the house. I saw a mist forming. It kept growing and swirling until it formed the shape of a woman. The face and features slowly took shape and became distinct. I realized, with a gasp, that I recognized the face from the old wedding photo. Even though I could see right through the vapor, I knew I was staring at the ghost of Lori!

When Julie turned to head for the door, she saw the spectral form and stopped in her tracks. A look of terror twisted her features while her mouth formed a circle of silent protest. As the phantom moved closer to Julie, she kept backing away, her eyes wide with horror. Her mouth working, Julie backed against the far end of the garage wall. I turned to watch her bump the handle of a shovel mounted directly above. The handle dislodged and the shovel fell from the wall and struck Julie on the head. Her body went limp as she fell to the floor. As she lay motionless, the mist floated past her and reached to open the garage door. Relief flooded through me when I saw the garage door slowly rise, letting fresh air into the garage.

I turned around and slumped against the seat, struggling against the growing lethargy enveloping me. My eyes felt heavy and I kept blinking, trying to stay awake. I was about to lose the battle when I heard a car drive up. I looked into the rear view mirror to see John get out of the car and run toward me.

"Karen!" I heard him cry.

Am I dreaming all this? I wondered. I heard the sound of running feet just before I lost the battle to stay awake. I felt as if I was slowly swirling until merciful blackness engulfed me.

What happened after that is hazy. I remember regaining consciousness briefly in the ambulance. Only fragments of what took place afterward remain. It wasn't until much later, when I fully regained consciousness and the danger was past, that John and I discussed what happened. John told me that he hadn't really been on the road, as he'd pretended.

"I took time off from work to rent a car and keep an eye on our house," he confided. "I wanted to find out who was coming in to disrupt the household, trying to make you doubt your sanity. Once I had proof, I was going to the police."

When he saw Julie come over, he waited, then decided he better check it out. She was his strongest suspect and he wanted to make sure I was all right.

Despite all the pain Julie had caused, John and I still felt pity for her. "Sometimes, Julie seemed almost too intense, but I had no idea that she felt anything for me," John confessed, his face pale and drawn.

Neither had I. Maybe the warning signs were there but we failed to see them. Living across the street from the man Julie thought she loved and seeing him every day must have been agonizing to her twisted mind. Maybe it drove her even further over the edge.

"Oh, Karen," John said, running his hands through his hair. "When I think of all the terrible things Julie did because of me. I feel that it's my fault."

I assured John that he wasn't to blame for the horrendous acts. "Julie is sick," I told him. "And Helen will see that she'll get the help she needs."

Tears flooded his eyes. "To think she killed Lori and almost killed you."

I reached up to caress his cheek. "At least, Alicia will no longer carry a burden of guilt."

Nodding, he took my hand in both of his.

I'll always be grateful that I stopped blaming Alicia for all that happened. Just as I'm thankful that I finally confided in my husband and he believed me. John had more faith in me than I did in him. I know, now, that love and trust go hand in hand. It's been a year, now, since that fateful morning. Helen moved away and Julie is still in a mental hospital. When she is declared mentally competent, she'll go to trial for murdering Lori and attempting to murder me.

I never told John about seeing Lori's ghost, for I felt that he and Alicia had endured enough. Besides, I felt certain her restless spirit would no longer be present in the house. I knew, somehow, that Lori was finally at peace.

Now that the nightmare is behind us, John and I have found that our love is even stronger. Free of guilt and nurtured by love, Alicia has truly blossomed and our home is blessed with happiness and peace. The only presence in our house, now, is one of hope and love. John, Alicia, and I—as well as a black and white cat named Checkers—are a true family, at last.

THE END

www.ingramcontent.com/pod-product-compliance
Lightning Source LLC
Chambersburg PA
CBHW071214130626
46555CB00004B/1705